A frenzied call of demonic triumph . . .

It filled Barrows's ears until he dropped to the ground, not believing what he heard, not believing what he saw, looking up despite his terror and seeing the nightbeast on the rock.

A wolf.

Huge, white, with staring amber eyes; huge, swaying, its claws already out and *scratching* slowly against stone; huge, panting, its fangs slicing the moon's surface when its head lifted again to bay.

Barrows scrambled for the rifle.

The wolf swung its head around.

Barrows couldn't find the

It licked its lips.

And sprang . . .

The Dark Cry of the Moon

CHARLES L. GRANT is an award-winning anthologist and author. His most popular novels are set in the eerie Connecticut town of Oxrun Station, and include *Hour of the Oxrun Dead* and *The Sound of Midnight*. He is also the editor of the blood-chilling *Shadows* series.

DON'T MISS CHARLES L. GRANT'S
CLASSIC NOVELS OF TERROR
—AVAILABLE FROM BERKLEY BOOKS . . .

THE SOFT WHISPER OF THE DEAD
AND
THE LONG NIGHT OF THE GRAVE

THE DARK CRY OF THE MOON

CHARLES L. GRANT

BERKLEY BOOKS, NEW YORK

This Berkley book contains the complete
text of the original hardcover edition.
It has been completely reset in a typeface
designed for easy reading and was printed
from new film.

THE DARK CRY OF THE MOON

A Berkley Book / published by arrangement with
the author

PRINTING HISTORY
Berkley edition / December 1987

ISBN: 0-425-10502-4

A BERKLEY BOOK ® TM 757,375
Berkley Books are published by The Berkley Publishing Group,
200 Madison Avenue, New York, NY 10016.
The name ''BERKLEY'' and the ''B'' logo
are trademarks belonging to Berkley Publishing Corporation.

PRINTED IN THE UNITED STATES OF AMERICA

10 9 8 7 6 5 4 3 2 1

AUTHOR'S DEDICATION

For Emily:
The only true princess
in a world too short of magic.

*Things happen in the Station, that's all.
Things happen. It's been that way from the
beginning . . .*

Lucas Stockton to his son,
Ned.
November, 1880

1

AUGUST, THE WAITING month: when the summer grows sullen and dampens the air, fills the lungs, dampens the spirit; when the trees are dimmed by veils of shifting haze, the leaves begin sagging, the bark is clammy and soft to the touch; when tempers are short and too weary to ignite, bodies are heavy no matter the weight, food is tasteless and drink is no redemption; when flesh is hot, cellars are dank, and the breeze is nothing more than a cruel jest of the sun.

August, the weary month: when those who must work do so in protest, taking out their frustrations on lathes and anvils, on counters and customers, on cloth and goldwork and the arc of a chair that would have been fine had it been crafted in June; and those on the streets complain of the weather, looking back on July when the sun seemed less oppressive, looking forward to September when memory tells

them there are genuine cool nights to enjoy on
the porch.

In the valley just below the slope of Pointer
Hill there were a half-dozen farms whose
fields were graveyards: dead stalks of har-
vested corn brown and broken across the furrows, acres dark and rocky and waiting dully
for spring. An occasional stand of oak to hold
timid shadows, a creek gone dry, the bones of
small fish scattered by hunting crows; a
nighthawk sweeping out of the forest, a colo-
ny of bats, the hooded yellow eyes of an owl
that waits.

A dog barks hysterically until its owner
throws a rock.

A horse kicks at its stall until a plank splin-
ters.

A footstep in the dark.

A stable, wide doors open, released a pulsing orange light as a bellows hissed air into a
red-steaming forge.

A shadow, huge on the plank wall, shim-
mered an arm high over an immense head,
slowly, slowly, poised while the shadow
burned into the wood.

Elijah MacFarland stood over his anvil and
brought his hammer down. The sound of iron
striking iron made him grin as he grunted in
time to his work—iron on iron, quick-tap-tap-
pound, until he regripped the tongs and held
up the sword. A nod, a frown, and he twisted
the blade back into the coals, pumped the
bellows and watched as the grey dust turned
red, turned orange, turned white. Iron on

iron, quick-tap-tap-*pound*.

He wore a pair of besmeared and grimy coveralls, he needed nothing more. He was bald, his massive chest gleaming blackly with sweat, arms thick as his anvil bulging as he lifted the hammer again.

Quick-tap-tap-*pound*.

It would have been awful nice to go into the village tonight, to the Chancellor Inn for some ale, to talk to the men and laugh for a change. They didn't mind at all he wasn't their color; that was the way of them. When he'd arrived last year from Hartford by way of Tennessee to work for George Tripper, not a one of them had bound him in an abolitionist banner—they could tell he'd been free the moment he dropped out'n his mother. Learned his trade early, and decided to make him a fortune makin crap for the ladies and garbage for the men—fancy brackets and curly fences, candelabra and fretwork, all done by an artist who had tamed a wild forge.

He checked the blade again, then whirled and plunged it into a tall vat of water. Steam rose (shadow steam writhed), made him blink away sweat while he took the blade out again slowly. A nod, a frown, and he sniffed as he dropped the long-handled tongs and sat on a high stool behind a whetting stone.

Lord, he was tired! Workin five days without rest, there bein a sad need of fine carvers for the Harley Regulars bound for Maryland next week. He reached into a long narrow box and pulled out a piece he had done the day before, held it up to the lantern light, and his teeth shone in a smile.

Fine, he thought; Elijah, you done just fine. This little beauty gonna make mince of someone's throat.

There were fancy thin swords for wearing to dinners and fancy engraved swords for wearing with plumes. But Elijah made killing edges, meant to slash, not to stab.

Elijah MacFarland made only sabres.

He set the water to dripping on the large round stone, put his feet on the pedals and started to hone. A touch of pressure here, a slight turn there, pulling back now and then to polish the sabre with soft cloth.

Quick-tap-tap-*pound* while he hummed four or five of his favorite hymns. Hummed until he heard, out in the dark, something moving.

Young Jeddy Tripper was never so glad to get out of the house in his life. He stood shivering in the dark of the back porch and listened to the whining, the scraping, the sudden shrill of a new sabre being shaped and sharpened, and he smiled to himself.

Even with the sun down, the moon on the rise, it was misery out here, but it was better than being in the kitchen with his father, listening to him whining about how he had to run the rundown farm by himself, telling his youngest son he weren't no good at all. Jeddy wasn't big, much too small for his ten years, and Father made him feel like it was all his fault that he couldn't top his brothers now fighting in the war. *Boy,* he would say out of that cavernous bearded mouth, *boy, you got some nerve not growin at all, I think the Lord decided you shoulda been a gopher.* And if Jeddy dare cry, he would look up from his stone jug, his eyes funny and nearly crossed, and tell him to grow up, be a man, stop whimpering like a pup who can't pee.

Elijah, on the other hand, keep tellin him he was somethin special, that the Lord don't make mistakes.

"Jed," he said once, "you look at me, go on, look. You ever seen such a mess in your life? But the way I figger, there was a purpose for this hulk, and I found it when I wasn't no more older than you."

Jeddy didn't understand that at all. Elijah wasn't a mess by anyone's imagination, he was magnificent. Tall as Pointer Hill and twice as wide, he could lift his anvil and carry it across the barnyard without half sweating, stop for a moment to wipe his brow and carry it right back. He'd seen the man lift a horse, and he'd seen him take one of his sabres and split a young hickory with it as if it were an axe.

Magnificent he was, and Jeddy knew he wouldn't mind if he stood by and watched the blades pounding into shape.

The ground was chilled beneath his bare feet when he stepped off the porch. He shuddered, wiped his palms on his baggy trousers, and headed for the stable, while the first round of the moon made its way skyward.

White; it was dead white, and it turned everything dead grey.

Elijah muttered as he slid off the stool and swung the sabre at his side. He'd been hearing sneakin around noises for an hour now, and he suspected it was one of them ruffians Chief Stockton had thrown out of town just the week before. Soldiers they were, home on the mend, soldiers gone bad 'cause they couldn't hold a job.

One was back now, probably wantin to steal some food. But ain't no damned ruff gonna play games with him.

He walked to the doors, smelling the hay and the manure and the sweat on his chest, not seeing his shadow sprawled on the stable wall. He leaned out, peering, searching for telltale shadows, listening for clumsy footsteps, the sabre swinging deadly just above the ground.

"C'mon," he muttered. "Damn you, c'mon or get outta here."

When the ruff didn't show, he walked to the fence bordering the road that lead back toward the village.

The moon was up, the night the color of early dying.

Suddenly he saw him, standing on the verge, watching him, daring him, and not making a sound. And Elijah MacFarland, who weighed eighteen stone, backed away from the fence, swallowed, and hefted the sabre high to his shoulder, remembering how strong he was, remembering that this blade was one he'd forged himself.

He saw it.

And he screamed.

Jeddy couldn't move. He'd never heard a man scream before, and he didn't know what to do. It was Elijah, it had to be, and he half-turned toward the house, to run and get his father. But Tripper was drunk, sleeping at the kitchen table, and Jeddy knew only that his only friend was in trouble.

He ran.

He ran to the stable and skidded around the corner, grabbing the door edge and looking inside.

It was empty. The forge was dying, the whetstone was still, and there was no sign of the black man, no sign at all.

Then he heard it, there on the other side of the building, near the fence. An odd noise he didn't recognize until he started creeping toward it, through the light to the dark, and then he knew what it was.

The moon was high, and he could see it all without squinting—Elijah spreadeagled on his back near the fence, and there was something straddling him, its pale muzzle turning red as its red fangs burrowed into Elijah's open chest. Burrowed, and ate, until it sensed Jeddy watching.

The head lifted.

Jeddy saw something red gently clamped in its jaws, something dripping, red, and pulsing.

It growled, and fixed him with darkbright

amber eyes.

It growled, and Jeddy felt his legs give beneath him.

George Tripper heard the scream, and thought it was his wife come back to haunt him. He groaned and clawed a trembling hand roughly through his beard. The second scream was louder, and he realized he was still in his kitchen, remembered yellin at Jeddy, and the boy tearin out of the house, slammin the door behind him.

Jeddy! Jesus God, Jeddy's in trouble.

He jumped away from the table, fell over his chair and banged his head on a cupboard door. He swore, staggered to his feet, and as he gripped the pump by the sink he heard the scream again.

He was drunk, and he knew it, and was proud of the way his legs carried him to the door, the way his hands grabbed the musket from its pegs on the wall. He couldn't run right, but that was okay; he moved in a fast shamble that took him toward the stable.

It's all right, Jeddy, I'm comin, I'm comin.

He tripped on a shadow and sprawled on the ground, the musket flying from his weak grip and sliding into the dark. His head felt as if it had been split to the core, and he whimpered as he pushed to his hands and knees and fumbled around for the weapon.

It was quiet now. No screaming. The sound of air in his lungs like the sound of bubbling water.

He shook his head to clear it, gave up on the musket and hobbled toward the fence, used it to prop him up while he watched the stable pass to his right, slowly, deserted, not a sign of anything, anyone moving.

"Jeddy!" he called. "Elijah!"

Not a sound.

He reached the corner and began moving parallel to the road.

"Jed, damn you boy, answer me!"

The moon nearly blinded him.

"Elijah, you black sonofabitch, where the hell are you?"

He tripped again, and put his hands out to catch himself, and looked straight down into what remained of Elijah's broad face, into the mangled cavity that had once been his chest. He shrieked and leapt to his feet, backed away with his head shaking. He licked at his lips, wiped his hands on his shirt and saw Elijah's blood smearing down to his stomach.

"Jed! Oh God, Jeddy!"

He didn't stop moving until he reached the stable door, looked around once and bolted inside. As he ran past the forge he grabbed a sabre from the table, spinning, watching shadows, trying to see where Jeddy had gone. Doves in the eaves cooed and fluttered, mice in the straw scuttled out of their sleep. The only horse he owned kicked at its stall, snorting, whickering, until Tripper reached the door, flipped the latch and let it out.

"Jeddy! Jeddy, goddamnit!"

He grabbed the roan's mane and drew himself onto its back, his thighs and knees gripping as he urged it outside.

The moon was higher, the yard clear, the field beyond.

The smell of fresh blood tossed the roan's head, but Tripper forced it around the barn, around the yard, through the shadows, whispering his son's name now, and cursing the jug that made him so damned dizzy.

Jeddy was gone. Elijah was dead. Tripper brandished the sabre at the nightsky, the moon, and heard a faint burst of music from the Barrows place, far across the field.

"Jeddy!" he shouted, and gave the roan its head, leaning low over its neck, swordarm hanging at his side, feeding fear with fear when he heard the first cry.

It began as a bark, rose to a wail, rose to a baying that froze the moon in its place and raised the dead from their graves.

Hungry.

Triumphant.

And less than ten yards away.

It coiled about his shoulders, brought ice to his blood, made him look around wildly until he was through the gate and on the dirt road.

He would have to go to the Barrows place.

He needed help; he needed saving; and when he could find no decent break in the stone, he cried out his frustration and forced the roan to jump.

The wall was low, the moonlight deceptive, and the horse caught its hind legs on the irregular top. It twisted, and George fell sideways, his shoulder striking a rock as he landed on the verge. The roan was shrieking.

He struggled painfully to his feet and looked over, saw the animal battling to rise, but its rear legs were useless.

"Jesus!" he shouted.

And heard the baying again, almost like laughing.

He stumbled away, the roan dropping from view, and his head would not stop shaking when he heard the *snap* of something's jaws, and the *crush* of bones, and the sudden deep silence that fell over the night.

Jeddy, dear God, Jeddy, what's happened to you?

And when it stood on the wall, all he could do was weep.

August, the waiting month, when the heat and the night scorched the soul black.

August, the weary month, when darkbright amber eyes never blinked on the way to their home in Oxrun Station.

2

IT WAS, WHEN it moved, more a shade than
something alive, buried in the dark under
overhanging branches that turned the center
of Williamston Pike into a Stygian tunnel.
Swiftly, yet without haste, it padded toward
the village. Tantalizing glimpses of an unearthly white flared when a bold moonlight
shaft found a break in the foliage and caught
the almost-shadow in its passing; discomfort-
ing glints of deep amber flashed like cursed
topaz when the shadow-thing's head swung
side to side, checking the Pike's shoulders for
signs of watching.

It saw (as if through cold amber fire) a
mastiff raise its head when it passed a closed
iron gate over which were the words, Squires
Manor. The mastiff tested the air, began instantly to whine, to back away from the gate
and claw feverishly at the ground.

Farther down, it saw (through flaming

amber) a monstrous black hound patroling
the gates of the Toal estate, a black hound
that caught its blood-scent, and began to
whimper. The hound dropped onto its side
(while the mastiff began barking) and exposed its belly, licking itself, urinating, panting so hard its head slammed against the
ground.

It saw (through amber) a flock of crows
suddenly lift from the trees (while the hound
began barking, the mastiff began howling)
and scream through the moonlit night.

The padding slowed as it approached an
intersection.

The padding stopped when it reached the
end of the park.

Only a pause before it moved again, the
amber fading, the padding fading.

There were footsteps now, and they were
walking assuredly along the darkened empty
pavement of Centre Street.

A flake of dried blood swayed to the ground.

Jerad Pendleton muttered and stumbled off
Doc Webber's porch on High Street and cursed
the day he'd met his wife. She'd come at him
full speed only an hour before with the flat
end of her skillet, shrewing and yelling about
his visits to the tavern, accusing him of whor-
ing, complaining that his salary from Bartlett's stables was barely enough to keep the
bank from their door and how were they supposed to take of poor Johanna while she
waited for a husband. He poked gingerly at
the bandage the doc had put on him, a cotton

wrap around his forehead that made him feel like some foreign prince; the wound stung and burned, and he winced, and decided that as long as the old witch was going to blame him for something, it might as well be for something good.

Doc Webber thought it was funny.

Jerad groaned at the headache stampeding through his skull and headed west for Centre Street.

Hell, it wasn't his fault he was celebratin, was it? Wasn't everybody in the village? There was a free-for-the-askin ale at the Inn, and it seemed like every house had somethin goin once the day was done. And why not, he wanted to know. Why the hell not? After all, it's not every day a war hero comes back to Oxrun in one piece, not every day anyone comes back from the War at all.

Christ, it was hot!

Besides, he knew Lawrence Drummond, knew him well. Tended his father's garden well enough, polished and scrubbed the sick old man's carriage while the old bastard was away even though it weren't his job, watched the old lady wither and die when her little boy took off to fight the Rebs. Hell, a man was entitled to let folks know how happy he was after all the grief, the killin, the boxes he'd seen in the mail car on its way to Hartford.

A crime, that's what it was; and a worse one when he saw Mister Larry step out of the train coach just four days ago, just four hours ahead of his gallivantin brother.

Christ, he must've aged a hundred years

down there. His brown hair was streaked grey, his face thin, his left arm in a sling, and a crutch propped under his right to hold him up. Jerad found out later, at the Inn, that Mister Larry had been at Shiloh just last April, had caught a minie ball in the ankle that had shattered the bone. Couldn't walk a lick without he had that stick of white pine jammed into his armpit.

Damn, what a crime.

Damn, it was hot.

At the corner he paused to let the headache do its work while he puffed for a breath. If he headed south to Chancellor Avenue he'd be on the way to the Inn and some solace for his aches; if he crossed right over he'd be headin home and no tellin what the old witch had up her sleeve.

He spat on his palm, clapped his hands, watched the spray.

South it was, then, and the hell with the old bat.

Past darkened shops, in and out of trembling streetlamps whose gas burned a faint gold, a faint blue, while the hot night air pressed his white homespun shirt against his lanky back. His boots cracked on the pavement, his shadow slithered alongside, and he could hear beyond the stores, in the houses, laughter, music, a town gone mad just because a boy come home.

A boy who looked as if he had walked hand in hand with Death, and Death cast him away; a boy who took several disturbing minutes before he recognized Jerad and shook his hand at the depot. Jerad had grinned; the boy's hand was deathly cold.

No surprise there. War does that to a man. He'd seen it in his own Dad when the old man came back from fighting the British in Canada before Washington was burned. Never said a word from a moment he walked in the door, right arm gone at the elbow, right eye a vacant hole. Never another word until the day he died.

Lordy, he thought, and shook himself like a wet dog, crossed the street and hurried past the white clapboard police station. His shoulders hunched, his stride lengthened, and he was near to Devon Street and the Inn when he heard footsteps behind him.

He peered over his shoulder.

Mist drifted out of the trees, settled on his stringy hair.

His right hand bunched into a fist. You couldn't be too careful these days, you sure couldn't. For every hero like Mister Larry who came home, there was a dozen more, ruffians, cutthroats, scoundrels angry at the world and takin it out on every man what moved. They didn't have much of a trouble with that here, not until a few days ago when a band of them had wandered right up the middle of Centre Street, terrorizing the ladies, snatching watches from the men. Would've been terrible, too, hadn't it been for Lucas Stockton. A giant of a man not known for his temper. A policeman. He had waded singlehandedly into those ruffs and pounded their heads into mush, hauled them off to the station and made them sleep it off two days before personally seeing to it they found their way out of town.

Can't be too sure, no sir, he thought as he checked the man coming toward him, lurching slightly, finally leaning heavily against a tree.

Jerad grinned. Nothing to worry about here; it was only a fellow imbiber.

He retraced his steps, one hand out for assistance before he saw the man's face.

"Good Lord in heaven above," he exclaimed with a quick look around to be sure no one else had spotted him. Then his voice dropped to a scolding whisper. "What are you doin out here? You ain't supposed to be here, you know that. Good heavens, don't you have any sense a'tall?" He grabbed the man's unprotesting arm and led him across the street, away from the Inn, toward the man's home.

"Lord, you're a terrible sight, if you don't mind me sayin so. What an awful sight. If you'd be me, my wife'd do more than take the skillet to your skull." He laughed, and pointed at the already bedraggled bandage around his head. "Lord, this is somethin, really somethin."

They turned left at the Northland Avenue corner, and moved down the quiet street to a large white house set back behind an iron fence much too elaborate for the land it enclosed.

"Lord," Jerad muttered, fumbling with the gate latch. "Lord, the lights is still on, they must be lookin all over for you. Tell you what

—I'll tell em you was with me, we had a bit too much, and I was helpin you walk it off. Sound okay? They ain't gonna know any better, sure as hell not."

The latch came unstuck. The gate creaked inward. Jerad turned to help the man through, and fell back against the fence.

But not fast enough to keep the claws from ripping through his throat.

"I have always been a damned reasonable man," Lucas Stockton insisted good-naturedly, waving an arm so wildly the rest of his companions at the bar had to duck to avoid having their heads taken off. "I am as reasonable as they come, and then some."

Laughter made him scowl, despite the fact that he knew it was done kindly, even affectionately. He didn't much care for being joshed. It smacked of lack of respect. It smacked of people trying to get on his good side because of his size, and because of his new position. And today, tonight, respect was finally his after years of study and patient work, years of attempting to give something to the Station in return for all it had given him.

Today the village council had appointed him the first chief of police.

Yet he wasn't foolish enough to think that rousting that gang had nothing to do with it.

"My dear sir," said portly Oliver Crenshaw, barely able to stand, his four-in-hand askew and his frockcoat pushed back by one imperious hand, "you are not reasonable. You are . . . you are beyond reason. You are—"

"Drunk," someone called from the front of the large room.

Crenshaw wheeled about, blinking, his thick blonde hair blinding him until he clawed it away. "Who said that?" he shouted. "Lucas, I demand you arrest that man! It's slanderous, that's what it is! How dare he speak to the authorities in that boorish manner."

Lucas shook his head and hunched himself over his tankard, wishing he had taken his own advice and stayed home with Ned and Mrs. Andropayous. His housekeeper had fixed the three of them a lavish meal, had even despite her inclinations placed a decanter of brandy on the table for the toast. But when it was over, Ned, already a strapping fifteen, had asked the old woman for a story about the way it was in her homeland. Lucas had smiled, pleased that the boy took his learning where he could, and came over to the Inn to see his old friends.

Thinking, a little wistfully, how pleased they would be at the appointment.

They were, in their own way—they jeered and teased and let him pay for nothing, and were not quite the same friends as he had that morning, before the meeting. Not quite the same, a little more distant.

He wondered if Johanna Pendleton would feel the same way.

His head buzzed, his hands stiffened from holding the pewter tankard for so long without lifting, without drinking, and he recognized the signs—time to leave, to head home and let

Mrs. Andropayous crawl into her own bed.

Hell, he thought, why the hell couldn't Madeleine be alive to see me? Why hadn't he the nerve to call on Johanna?

It took him over an hour to leave the crowded, dark-paneled room, to accept mocking condolences and sincere handshakes, to break out the door and stand in the street to breathe the muggy air. His shadows cast from the two lanterns either side of the entrance crossed like sabres on the pavement, doubling his six-and-a-half feet, tripling his two hundred pounds. He grinned. It was impressive, he had to admit it—a giant of a man, he announced to himself; a giant that bestrides the streets of Oxrun Station with the vigilance of a god.

"Oh lord," he groaned, though not entirely unhappily. "Oh lord, I'm drunk."

He started to whistle, the first few bars of 'All Quiet On The Potomac Tonight' so out of tune he shut himself up.

The foliage shifted, husking damply. The scrape of his soles on the pavement rasped too loudly.

"Drunk," he whispered.

And his voice was the only sound he could hear in the dark.

Immediately, not liking what the ale had done to his nerves, he swung around the corner and headed up Devon as fast as he could without actually running, to the small red-brick cottage where Ned was born, where Madeleine had died; he stopped on the porch, turned and looked back at the street, at the sleeping village it represented.

His. By damn, it was his for the protecting.

Then he heard the baying.

It came from his left, on the other side of the Avenue, rising sharply above the trees toward the waning full moon. He listened, puzzled, first thinking it nothing but a dog until the baying rose again, deep and imperious, claiming the moon for its own. He squinted, and brushed a hand down over his coat. It was a wolf, by god, no question about it. Probably over in the woods down beyond King Street.

A third time, that set off every dog in town; not angry, not joining, but a terrified howling that brought a chill to his spine and a crawling dread that broke his arms out in gooseflesh. He swallowed, wishing it were the drink that made his throat abruptly dry.

It was an odd time of year for wolves to be prowling so far south, so near humans; he listened, and did not hear the door open behind him.

"Jesu Cristu," a quavering voice whispered.

He looked around at the old housekeeper and saw her clutching a wooden cross.

3

"YOU DO NOT listen to me," Maria accused, giving him a stare that made him feel ten years old. Her unidentifiable accent was not as thick as it had been eight years ago, but it sounded worse whenever she lost her temper, or decided her fragile pride had been deliberately injured. "And what do I know, eh? I'm just an old dying woman you pulled in off the streets. A charity. I give you a reason for God to be pleased."

"Maria, for heaven's sake." Exasperation closed his eyes, turned one hand to a loose fist. She was a wonderful woman, no question about it, but there were times when he wished she would give her tongue and temper a rest. "This is all nonsense. You are not a charity, and I don't care if God is pleased for it or not."

"Blasphemy," she accused.

He nodded, accepting the condemnation mutely, knowing another word would bring a scathing sermon down on his aching head.

They were inside, he seated at the bare oak kitchen table. A fire in the stove defeated the open back door, a kettle boiling on the grate made him sweat just thinking about it. But he said nothing, not the way she was behaving since they had returned from the porch. He leaned back in his chair, unbuttoned his shirt, and watched the tiny woman bustling about, muttering to herself, every so often slapping a hand against her brown skirts.

"You know me," she grumbled. "I never dream. I never tell lies. You know me. Now you think I am ready to go to the mountains, to die."

He threw up his hands, looked to the ceiling for support.

"That's all right," she said stoically. "It is fine that I am old. I will not burden you much longer."

"Maria, you're going to live forever. What's all this talk about dying, for god's sake."

"You are Chief of all the police now. You have to know about such things."

"I think I know a little about dying, don't you?" he said, reminding her of how she'd come to be with him and his son in the first place.

"That is one thing, that is a natural death," she said, turning at the stove to fix his gaze with her black eyes. "This is something new. Something you will have to learn about, Lucas, and you are not going to like it."

He smiled. She was incredible, Maria was. From the neck down she was wrinkled and wattled and spotted with age, with less weight on her than a chicken, with more force in those tiny lungs than the worst storm he'd ever heard. But her face was what marked her, and what made him choose her from all the applicants after Madeleine had died of the fever in '52, ten years ago, when Ned was only five.

It was a smooth face, lean and dour, touched by deep black eyes blacker for the solid crown of white that passed for her braided hair. Age was there, but no creases; tragedy was there, but no tears.

It was, for all it had suffered, a beautiful face.

And Maria, he thought, was a beautiful woman.

She spoiled his son unmercifully and ruled Lucas like a tyrant and from the third anniversary of Madeleine's death had a sedate, proper, but earnest procession of young women in by her own invitation, ostensibly for Sunday dinner, and belaying her Romany background by virtually turning down the bed whenever he mentioned in passing Johanna Pendleton's name.

Tonight, however, she was more on edge than he'd ever seen her. Hot water slopped from the cups, ran unchecked across the counter; the cups rattled in their saucers; the saucers hit the table so hard they almost broke.

A welcome breeze talked to the leaves in the yard, slipped inside and caught briefly at her hair.

"By God, Maria, you've got to calm down," he complained when she looked fearfully at the open door. "I heard it too, you know. It's only a wolf, nothing to be afraid of."

She managed a twisted smile; a breeze sifted in and whisked around her skirts.

"Sit down," he ordered kindly. A sweep of his hand captured the brandy, and he laced both cups liberally, astonished when she did not complain. Then his gruff manner softened. "I imagine it brings back memories, that creature out there."

Maria hesitated before nodding, sipping at the potent tea as if it were iced cold.

"I would guess," he continued when she appeared disinclined to talk, "that the mountains there are filled with them. I guess you saw them all the time."

Another nod, less tentative.

He waited, hoping she would give him an answer, launch into one of her old-country stories that would take her mind off the howling.

She said nothing; her left hand protected her cup with a palm while her right caressed the wooden cross now dangling from a leather thong around her neck.

"Maria?"

"The wolf is a hunter."

At last, something. "He is that, when he's hungry."

Her lips pursed, seemed to vanish, the veins on the backs of her hands bulged darkly and seemed to throb.

"This one," she said, "is more than just hungry."

The night returned to silence.

The dogs stopped their barking, returned whimpering to their sleep.

On Northland Avenue darkbright amber eyes focused on the bulge of the moon, watching as it made its way down toward the horizon, stretching bare branches into shadows against the stars, filling crowns and shrubs with a brief preternatural glow.

It watched, and licked its lips, and as the amber faded, as the greylight returned, the smells faded with it: the fresh grass and the tang of the leaves, the old brown cloth of the drunk man's coat, the acrid bite of his worn boots, the fear-scent of his sweat. And the salty sweet aroma of the spill of his blood.

Taste faded as well: the rough and scratchy bits of shirt in its mouth, the after-taste of ale spilled over the cloth, the break of flesh, the bite of bone . . . and the smooth pulse of the heart as it made its way down its throat.

Taste faded, but did not die.

Now it was full; tomorrow it would be hungry.

And it didn't mind a bit.

Constable Farley Newstone took his time walking up Northland Avenue. His dark uniform tunic was unbuttoned, his hair in mild disarray. At the moment he was busily refastening his collarless shirt and hoping no one was watching from back of the curtains. Behind him, on King Street, with its back to the woods beyond, was a small clapboard house with a woman just returning to her empty bed. No doubt she would be thinking about him, about the way he had handled her and how she had begged him wildly for more. He would have surrendered to the plea just to see the gratitude in her eyes, but her husband was due home and he didn't want to be the one to hurt poor Charlie's feelings.

He had left, then, with a loud kiss and a silent promise, and was fumbling back into his wrinkled uniform and grinning to himself, still feeling of the hot touch of her on his palms and praying that stupid old Charlie would take the night tour again tomorrow. Charlotte hadn't exactly sworn that she would see him, but he knew her too well. She would, all right. She couldn't get enough of him. She would see him without a doubt, and he'd leave her begging again.

He laughed aloud, shook his head, and glanced automatically into the yards he was passing. As always, in Oxrun, there was nothing out of place.

A sigh of boredom, then, a final brass button slipped into its place. He pulled his walnut nightstick from its sheath at his hip and tapped it against his thigh impatiently.

No, there was nothing to see. There was never any damn thing to see around here. Not even in the overgrown wooded lot between the Crenshaws and the Drummonds. The Chief—and that was a laugh, now, wasn't it, that big ape a Chief, like he was in a city or something—the Chief wanted them to check everything these days, what with those ruffs prowling around and causing good folk a lot of trouble, and he supposed he should at least make a stab at checking the lot, but he didn't feel like tramping through weeds and tripping over roots, getting his new low boots dirty and having to pry burrs off his coat and trousers. Let someone else do it; he wanted to get back to the stationhouse and get himself some water.

A twirl of the nightstick, a soundless whistle, a wondering about the howling he had heard while he was with Charlotte. A dog crazy with the moon, or a wolf over from New York or down out of Massachusetts. To tell the truth, he didn't know the difference. He was from Boston, out of Springfield, and wouldn't know a wolf from a sheep dog if he fell over them at full noon.

Probably, he thought, it was goddamn Lucas celebrating his promotion.

He slipped, then, and scowled down at the brick pavement. Saw nothing and walked on, barely noting the Drummond house, not seeing the light flick off in the upper window.

Not noticing at all the blood drying on his new boot.

Lucas didn't know whether to scold the old woman, or humor her. She sipped at her tea, and he knew she tasted nothing, not even the strong brandy; she fingered the delicately wrought cross and muttered prayers to herself, and it was all getting to be much too much for the ale in his system and the rasping she was doing to his nerves.

For the first time since she'd joined him, he wondered if he had made a mistake.

"Maria," he said finally, reaching out and touching her arm, "this isn't Europe, remember? And we're not living in those old mountains of yours. All that's past. This is the United States. This is Oxrun Station, and you've nothing to be afraid of."

"You heard it," she said without looking up from her cup. "You heard the dogs."

He couldn't deny it. It was the most unnerving thing he'd ever heard in his life, and for a moment there he'd felt like taking his guns and putting them all out of their misery.

"You heard it. It hunts."

"No, not here," he assured her gently. "Too many farms, too much hunting. It isn't safe ground for them anymore, hasn't been for years. For the most part they stick to Canada and high New England. That one," and he nodded toward the backyard, "is either sick and dying, or too bold for his own good. He'll be dead by sunset tomorrow, I'll bet. Next week, some wife will have herself a new muff."

The breeze sent the gaslight to waving shadows on the walls.

A spark snapped in the stove, and made him jump with a muttered oath.

"Maria, did you hear what I just said?"

The housekeeper rose without speaking, poured the tea into the stone basin and returned to the table. Her eyes silenced what comment he might have made; her hands, quivering and pale, overturned the cup onto the saucer. She stared at the ceiling and muttered to herself, lifted the cup and examined the leaves brown and dark on the saucer.

"Ah," Lucas said, "gold headed our way? No." He leaned over his folded arms. "A woman. Dark, mysterious, loving of children and too much for me." He reached out and gripped her shoulder. "It's late Maria. I'm going to bed."

She said nothing.

The breeze filled the room with a welcome chill.

He was at the door when she spoke his name.

When he turned, she looked up.

"The wolf," she said, "walks on two legs."

4

AN ARMY OF flies hovered in a shimmering glittering cloud over the body of Elijah Mac-Farland. The sheet draped over him seemed to have no effect; it rippled, undulated, as the insects crept under the edges to concentrate on their feeding. The buzzing filled the barn obscenely.

Lucas stood outside, having seen enough of what was left of the only man in Oxrun as large as himself. In deference to the continuing heat, he was dressed in a loose white suit, but after hours of tramping over the barnyard, searching through the house, he had taken off tie and collar and jammed both into his jacket pocket. His thick brown hair curled over his forehead, and he swiped at it constantly to drive it from his eyes.

Several of his men, their faces red and their constables' uniforms darker with sweat stains, reported to him every few minutes, but none gave him the answer he sought.

A horse whickered, and he looked to his left, saw Doc Webber and his surgical assistant lifting George Tripper's body into the back of a wagon. Webber was complaining loudly, the assistant was stoic.

Not five minutes ago Webber and Lucas had stood on the house porch and watched the summer heat rising from the fields.

"'Course it was a critter," Webber had said grumpily. "You think some *man* could do that?"

"And the horse?"

"Beats me," was the somewhat puzzled reply. "Looks like George tried to jump the wall and missed. The animal's back legs were snapped. Whatever killed it caught it lying on the ground."

Webber was dressed in black from his rounded hat to his long coat and trousers. There wasn't a drop of perspiration on his puffed, flushed face.

"I heard a wolf last night," Lucas said.

"So that's what set the dogs going. God, thought I was going to have to lock myself in the morgue." He spat, shook his head. "Sure it was a wolf?"

"I know one when I hear one."

"That'll do it, then," Webber said. "Have t'be a damned big one, though, to bring poor Elijah down like that." Then he yelled at his assistant, who was struggling with Tripper's body. He leapt off the porch and skuttled into the road to grab the corpse's feet. Lucas followed slowly, stopping at the fence and listening to his men whispering to themselves, fingering once in a while the pistols they kept in holsters at their waists.

Welcome, Chief, they'd laughed when he walked in that morning; there were flowers in a vase in his new office, a large bottle of whiskey gaily wrapped on the desk, and a woven basket filled with calling cards wishing him well. He'd loved it. It made him feel on top of the world, a sensation that lasted only until Don Barrows came pounding in from his farm with news about the killings.

When he saw the bodies he nearly threw up.

When he couldn't find Jeddy, he had to fight to hold the panic.

Now he sniffed, wiped a hand over his face, and turned to the small open carriage that was his by right. He swung into it, beneath the overhanging half-roof, and took the reins. Charlie Notting ran up and clung to the side, grinning as he mopped a soaked handkerchief over his red-bearded face.

"You leaving?"

Lucas looked at the reins pointedly. "No, I think I'll beat the nag to death."

"Oh." Charlie frowned, and Lucas was almost sorry he had made the jest. Charlie, for all his fine qualities as a man and a policeman, was singularly humorless; a hard worker who would never rise very far but who would be stalwart, always willing, always volunteering to take the after-dark shifts—it was perhaps his stumbling way of covering his regret for having married Charlotte. And

that, he thought sympathetically, was a bad
match if there ever was one.

"Anything else," he asked kindly, in case
Charlie thought he was annoyed.

Charlie shrugged apologetically. "We
haven't found a sign of the boy, Mr. Stockton.
Nothing at all. If he's hiding, he's hiding good.
And if . . ."

He thought of Ned, and shuddered.

"By the way, Chief, Mr. Barrows wants to
know if you want a hunting party out."

He looked over to the barn. Don Barrows
was at least as heavy as he, and eight inches
shorter, glittering green suspenders barely
able to keep his trousers at the midpoint of his
rolling stomach. In his hand he held a Sharps
carbine. His four strapping sons stood beside
him, similarly armed.

"Won't hurt," Lucas said. "But be sure you
tell him—" He changed his mind, asked Charlie to fetch the farmer over.

Tell him what, he thought; to be careful?
Barrows already knew that, he'd seen what
the thing had done to MacFarland. He had
also sneered when Lucas let slip what Maria
had said the night before.

He was still sneering when he came over,
sons trailing, and leaned heavily against the
carriage.

"You want something, Chief?" The title was
an expletive; Barrows had wanted someone
more pliable for the part.

Lucas stared him down. "Yes, Don, I want
you and your boys to take one of my men with
you."

"What?" Barrows slapped the sidewall so hard the grey in the traces jumped. "Lucas, I can't do no real hunting with an idiot—"

"Charlie Notting will go. He can track, as you well know, and I need someone official there in case you find the boy. Besides," he added wryly, "I don't want you shooting anyone who might be dipping in a stream."

Barrows decided he was being funny, and laughed. "All right, Chief, all right."

Lucas tightened the reins, and the grey began to inch forward. "You know anything about wolves?"

"Wolves?" Barrows was disdainful. "Bear, y'mean." Then he remembered, and laughed again, shaking his head. "Lucas, that old woman of yours hasn't been outta the Station in a hundred years. She don't know a thing about what's in the woods around here."

"I heard it," Lucas reminded him flatly.

"Sure you did, sure you did. But that dog wasn't a wolf, and that dog didn't do to the nigger what was done, believe me."

Lucas didn't argue. It was too hot, and Barrows was too close. "You just be careful," he said. "And keep your eye out for sign of the boy."

"The boy," Barrows said as he turned on his heel, "is probably halfway to Virginia by now, screaming his head off."

Lucas doubted it, but said nothing. He sat as far forward as he could on the red cushioned seat and drove slowly, scanning the fields for signs of Jeddy Tripper.

* * *

It was just past noon, but already the night-beast could feel the pull of the full moon. Hunger made it impatient. It had only three days to feed itself for the rest of the month; three days to gorge, three days to feast on the delicacy of the heart.

It glanced around its room, and for a moment the furniture was tinted with dark amber.

It smiled, and nodded.

It blinked its wide eyes until the amber vanished, then opened the door and stepped into the hall.

Johanna Pendleton hated herself for feeling so out of place, and hated herself more for coveting all that she saw.

The foyer of the Drummond house was extensive, severly ostentatious for a house outside the estates that took the land behind the village park. Pedestaled Greek statuary, sober wall hangings, a floral-and-fringed carpet thicker than fresh grass, and the whole smelling to her of someone trying too hard.

She stood apprehensively with her back to the door. Her ivory blouse was frilled, collar lacey and high, voluminous skirts a spring green complementing the pale gold of her long, upwardly braided hair. She knew it was wrong, but still she was unable to shed the uncomfortable feeling that she had come here to beg, to ask permission of a plantation's Master.

It was silly, and her cheeks grew spots of red when her anger began to boil. She was only here to find her uncle, and if the Drummonds chose not to tell her she could always go to Lucas.

Footsteps interrupted her thoughts, and she looked up the long polished staircase.

Two men descended toward her, and she managed a bright smile when they spotted her, and nodded cheerfully.

Bartholomew Drummond was tall and slender, power in his shoulders, power in the way his pale blue eyes fixed on you and held you, turning you around, examining, and assessing; Lawrence, even with the burden of his crutch and his arm in its sling, was just as imposing, but in a more understated way. His own eyes were a darker blue, his weight concentrated in his chest and legs, his appeal coming from the sardonic twist of a smile that never left his thin lips.

Both were newly returned to Oxrun—Bartholomew from a Grand Tour through the countries of Middle Europe, Lawrence from the War.

Each took one of her hands before she could protest, and drew her into the sitting room where they flanked her, each in an armchair, while she was granted the Empire couch.

They chatted briefly for a while about the abomination called the weather—Bartholomew with flare, Lawrence cynically and quiet—before she was able to break in and ask about her uncle.

"Jerad?" Bartholomew said, a white-gloved finger pressed to his chin. "No, I don't believe

I've seen him all day. A shame, too; the roses are dying."

"You should check the Inn," Lawrence told her, his tone lacking concern. "Better place than this."

"He works here," she said tightly, "or had you forgotten?"

"You forget a lot of things in a war, Johanna."

Bartholomew had the grace to appear distressed, and deliberately putting his back to his brother he took her hand and guided her to her feet. "Pay him no mind," he said as they walked back to the door. "He likes feeling sorry for himself."

"Bart!" she scolded in a hushed whisper. "Larry was wounded! Nearly killed!"

"True," he said contritely. "But it's hard when all he ever talks about is death and dying."

The house had no porch, only an elaborately paned frame around the front door. She stepped down to the walk, and looked around. "Would you . . . I don't like to ask it, but would you mind terribly sending someone around if he should come? Aunt Delia is frantic."

"I shall come myself," he promised with a smile. "It has been a long time, Johanna."

"Indeed."

He looked over her head at the grounds beyond. "I must confess I still have . . . affection for you."

She lowered her gaze. "Thank you, Bart."

"But you haven't changed your mind."

"No. I'm sorry."

"No need," he said brightly. "I'll soon change it for you. In fact, if you've nothing planned, would you mind having luncheon with me this afternoon?"

She hesitated, not wanting to encourage him, and not wanting to seem too cool. "I . . . I do have my work, Bart."

"Fie!" he said good-naturedly. "Still a clerk in Crenshaw's shop are you?" When she nodded, he snapped his fingers. "Then you shall take your lunch with me. Oliver will be mollified, I assure you. A purchase for his coffers will make him forget you for the moment, at least." He took her hands, held them warmly. "In an hour? At the Inn?"

Past him, in the foyer, she could see his brother watching. Lawrence, who had courted her just as vigorously before he enlisted, and had refused to see her the day he returned home.

"Yes," she said. "In an hour."

Smiling broadly, he remained in the doorway until she was through the gate. A wave, and she touched a hand to her hair, felt the heat nesting there, and wished she'd brought her parasol. Little shade was better than none at all, certainly better than frying here on the street like one of Mrs. Andropayous's specially prepared eggs.

She reached Chancellor Avenue and stood beneath a richly crowned elm, debating whether to go report failure to her aunt, check the Inn as Larry suggested, or—

A carriage rattled out of Centre Street far to her right. It was Lucas, she realized, when

the new Chief climbed out and handed the
reins to the station's stable-boy. When he
glanced in her direction she lifted a timid
hand. He spotted her, and she saw the grin,
sighed her relief when he beckoned her over.

She couldn't stop herself; the moment she
reached his side she stretched and planted a
solid kiss on his cheek. A patrolman lounging
at the station door coughed into a fist and
disappeared inside. Lucas glowered, smiled,
finally turned away and watched the pedestri-
an traffic fill the streets.

"Congratulations," she said.

"Thank you," he muttered, trying not to be
obvious about brushing back his hair.

Then, through his delightful confusion, she
saw the look in his eyes. "Lucas, don't tell me
you have business already. On your first day?"

Sparing her the details, he told her about his
morning, and she felt briefly faint.

"Johanna?"

"My god, Lucas, Uncle Jerad hasn't been
seen since last night."

5

Before Lucas could respond, a grey-coated, goated man came up to them without apology for the interruption and demanded hotly to know what Stockton intended to do about the prowler in his yard the night before, the one that set off all the dogs in the state. Lucas politely confessed ignorance just as a second man and his wife approached them from behind, complaining loudly about the fearsome wild animal that had frightened their children to death last night with its ungodly howling, and what were they paying him for if it wasn't to keep a simple beast from invading the village.

Lucas smiled gamely, but it was no use. Within moments a small, vociferous crowd had gathered to lodge similar protests, and it wasn't long before he grabbed Johanna's elbow, smiled courteously and broadly, and pushed his way through to the station doorway. Once inside he brought her to his office, yelled instructions to the constable on duty to take down the complaints, then closed the door and sagged into his chair.

Johanna was struggling for composure, her hands clasped tightly in her lap. "They have a right to be worried," she said at last. "It sounded horrid, that thing did."

"I know," he admitted solemnly. "But I think that worry is misplaced as far as your uncle is concerned." He managed a twisted smile. "Jerad has been known to find a bush to sleep behind, Johanna, when he's had more than a few tots at the Inn, or in that shed behind the Drummond place."

"But he wasn't drinking last night," she said, and told him about the argument, the flying skillet, and Jerad's flight to the doctor's. A sentence, no more, about her visit to the Drummonds.

He sighed, more a grumbling deep in his throat. "You've seen our boys, then, home from their travels."

"That's not nice, Lucas. Larry was wounded badly."

"According to John Webber," he said, unrepentant, "Larry no more needs that sling than he does another pot of gold. It's sympathy he's after, if you ask me. Sympathy for a cripple since no one cares much for him any other way."

"Lucas!"

He shrugged an insincere apology. He had no use for either of the Drummonds. Their ailing father had made the family fortune, then took himself abroad to find cures for his sicknesses which, it was said, were considerably more than legion. In his absense, Bartholomew was unarguably diligent in keeping the financier's company profitable and was respected throughout the state as a worthy successor to the old man; in Lucas's view, however, he was still nevertheless a reprobate, known as well for invading the homes of half the widows and single women within three day's travel. His charm, of course, kept him out of trouble, but as far as Lucas was concerned, he was not much better than his more open brother.

Johanna giggled. He looked up, realized he was glowering, and forced his brow to smooth over.

"I think you're jealous," she teased.

"And I think you're out of line, young woman," he snapped.

She giggled again, and reminded him that out of line or not, she was still concerned about her uncle. Her aunt, she said, was ready to scalp him, especially after their fight the night before.

"Ah," he said, relieved she had changed the subject, relieved too that this, at least, was a simple domestic matter, "then he's hiding. I would too, if I were married to your aunt and she was after my scalp. A formidable woman Delia is, and you know that's the truth."

Her eyes lowered, but her lips quivered in a ghost of a smile. "She . . . can be intimidating, yes."

"Intimidating, hell, she ought to be in the

army. They could have used her at Seven
Pines."

The smile broke.

"Well, then," he said explosively, startling
her into looking up, "I'll have the boys keep
their eyes out. We'll have him back, no fear,
Johanna. Unless, that is, he comes crawling
back on his own."

She could not help a laugh. "Are you always
so positive, Lucas?"

"As positive as I have to be," he said wryly.
"When the occasion calls for it."

A sideways glance, and she rose, fanning
herself with one hand. "Devilishly hot. Lord, I
wish the weather would break."

"More tempers will before the temperature
does," he predicted, walking with her to the
door. He towered over her, but felt as though
they were the same height, a sensation he was
not sure he approved of, and definitely did not
understand.

A hand rested on his arm, and he covered it
with his own, snatched it back when he saw
the twinkle in her eye.

"You will find the boy, won't you?" she
asked.

"Of course. Barrows, for all his bluster, is a
good man, and Charlie's there to keep an eye
on him. Between the two of them, the lad'll be
in my hands by dark, you can be sure of it."

"Where will he go?" she wondered aloud,
stepping into the hall into the rolling voices
from the front. Before he could respond, she
turned and clasped his upper arm. "Lucas, he
has no family now, the poor thing. Bring him

to me. We'll take care of him."

"I'll consider that generous offer, Jo, believe me. You're a fine woman, a damned fine woman."

She flushed with embarrassment, had turned to leave when, on impulse, he asked if she were free to dine with him this afternoon. The look on her face made his stomach turn over.

"I'm sorry, Lucas," she said quietly. "I have promised to join Bartholomew at the Inn." She brightened for a moment. "I could always decline, you know. It would be—"

"No," he said. "It's all right. I was just . . . well, I'll probably not have the time anyway."

"But Lucas, really—"

He took her arm and turned her gently but firmly around, gave her a slight push. "Get on, Jo, before he thinks you've stood him by. Another time, if that's agreeable to you. When there's less trouble, and I know we won't be interrupted."

She took two paces down the hall, looked back and gave him a broad wink. A second one, and a come-hither roll of her shoulder made him clear his throat and pray no one was watching.

He was still standing there five minutes later, knowing he was smiling like an idiot, and not giving a damn, and hating the thought of Bartholomew Drummond holding her hand.

He was wrong about the weather.

A dark cloud was spotted shortly before

midafternoon. It climbed ominously over
Pointer Hill, a boiling grey frigate whose keel
churned black, spreading to obliterate what
blue there was, what sun there was, splitting
aside the heat with the thunder of its black
prow. The wind kicked, gusted, spun more
than a few parasols out of astonished hands
and into the streets, flapped awnings like
desperate wings, spawned dust devils in the
gutters that sent horses to rearing and chased
yelping dogs to cover.

The temperature dropped.

Shadows forged edges as sharp as blades.

In the distance there was thunder.

Farley Newstone had just about had it with
whining women and red-faced men. The poor
dogs were doing this, the cursed dogs were
doing that, my god you'd think the whole
world was coming to an end just because
some hound got it into his skull to bay at the
moon.

He sat the front desk and scribbled nonsense on the report sheets Stockton had com-
manded be written for each complaint. They
were all the same anyway; he would copy
them over later. Right now, he was peeved at
not being on the streets. The wind was blow-
ing cool, and he could feel its salvation whenever the doors opened and someone else
entered with fire and brimstone in their eyes,
and acid on their tongues. He wanted to be out
there, reveling the coming rain, watching the
dimming light, preparing himself for a quick
visit to Charlotte as long as Charlie was busy

keeping Don Barrows in line.

The noise in the room grew.

His collarless tunic seemed tighter than usual.

Suddenly he could stand no more. At the top of his voice he ordered them all back of the railing, take a seat, he'd be with them in a minute, thank you very much for your patience.

Then he rose, held up the ink pot to show them all it was empty, and ducked into the storeroom to his left, closed the door and leaned against it. His eyes shut momentarily. A hell of a day. First there was waking to the furnace outside, then finding blood of all things on his brand new boot. It had taken him an hour to polish it off, and even now, when he looked down, he thought he could see the stain spreading from the sole, up over his heel.

And once he had seen the crowd inside, and once Stockton had grabbed his arm and shoved him behind the high desk on the platform, he had prayed that Charlotte would be in top form tonight.

Then thunder rattled the building, and he bit down on his lower lip. Too hard. He tasted blood, and immediately began gagging.

The Inn was uncrowded, the dining rooms upstairs elegant in their simplicity. The casement windows were open to the cool breeze, and linen napkins fluttered on the square maple tables. A waiter hovered by the staircase landing, another carried a tray of wine glasses down the back stairs to the kitchen.

Johanna sat nervously, watching as Bart finished his brandy and slumped with a sigh in the high-backed chair. His pale eyes had not left her once, and though she was flattered, she could not help a constant comparison between the financier and the chief of police; Aunt Delia would be horrified, she thought, to know who had won out.

Still, it was better than being in the shop, ducking away from Crenshaw's grasping, pinching fingers, straining smiles at the matrons who fluttered in, and fluttered out, treating her as if she were less than the straw their carriage horses ate. For a time she was able to relax, to listen to Bart's marvelous stories of his trip abroad, how he suffered a mild affliction that forced him to temporarily wear kid gloves, and grin at the strange customs he had come across in his travels.

"And is one of those customs," she said with a laugh, "not eating your lunch?" The serving girl had taken away almost a full plate, and he had chosen not to taste any of the fresh fruits or candied sweets.

"It is the custom of my stomach," he said with a slap to his abdomen. "I seldom eat out, and my stomach knows it."

"Then—"

"Because of you, my dear," he said gallantly. "It has been a while since I've spent time with someone as delightful as you."

"Bart, please," she said, glancing around to see if anyone had overheard.

"But it's true!" he protested gaily. "Good Lord, Johanna, I've thought of you daily since leaving this place."

"You didn't write," she told him.

He was abashed, and looked away. "I know only figures, my dear. Letters are quite beyond me."

"A note, then."

A sideways glance. "You're teasing."

She covered a grin with her hand. "A little."

"And flirting?"

Her eyes widened. "Sir, you presume!"

"Indeed I do, Johanna. It is how I manage to keep the fortune going despite my brother's expenses."

She sobered, and scolded him for his constant carping at Larry, reminding him of the man's sacrifices and in the same tone accusing him of possibly using the trip as an excuse not to join the fighting. A faint line creased his brow, and he would have retorted angrily, she was sure, but a sudden peal of thunder made the glasses sing. He jumped, almost stood, and a sheen of perspiration broke across his brow.

"Bart, are you all right?"

He took a deep swallow of water, mopped his brow with his linen, and finally nodded. "Startled me, that's all."

She didn't believe him, and seeing himself exposed, he merely shrugged and asked the waiter for an accounting. When the sum was achieved and the money paid, he rose and took her elbow, guided her down the stairs and out the door.

"May I escort you back to the shop?" he asked, though he clearly did not mean it.

"No, Bart," she said. "Just . . ."

He watched her closely. "Is it your uncle?" And shook his head when she shook hers. "Ah." He slipped his hands into his trouser pockets and rocked his heels. "The Drummonds, am I correct? Ardent swains once, now mysteriously cool and distant. You wish to know what has happened."

"I am curious," she admitted.

"It is best you don't know," he said after a long moment. "I would only repeat that my affection for you has not dimmed, and it won't be long before I'm . . . before I'm my old self again."

He leaned over and kissed her then, just as Lucas came round the corner.

6

THE ROOM ON the second story was small. Once used for sewing, all the carpetbags and material chests had been removed to make room for a narrow wardrobe and a plain brass bed. The only window was tall and narrow, scarcely more than a slit in the blank white wall, framed by white curtains now gone yellow and brown with dust and age. Beside it was a rocking chair, its back covered by a faded patch-quilt that dangled limply to the floor.

A man sat there, staring blindly into the backyard. His alarmingly thin legs were buried beneath a lumpy mound of worn blankets without color; his frail arms, more sticks than limbs, poked out of a brown jacket much too small for his size. He wore slippers whose soles were in dire need of a cobbler, a sweater so thin it seemed part of his soiled shirt.

He coughed violently, and the chair rocked.

Tears of pain filled his rheumy eyes, slid
down harshly creased cheeks, dropped from a
jaw too sharp at the chin. He sighed, and
coughed again, strands of dirty white hair
falling over his brow.

He spat phlegm into an already darkened
handkerchief, and leaned back to gulp for
air.

A glass of tepid water sat on a rickety table
beside the bed. It was too far to reach; it had
been years since he had walked.

As the afternoon light slipped away ahead
of the racing cloud, his fingers began to jump.
One. Another. As if trying to leave the parchment hands and reach for the bell cord that
hung just out of his reach. The chair rocked in
sympathetic time to his frustration; the rock-
ers squeaked over the carpet, in time to the
meaningless cries that slipped between blood-
less lips.

And when the door finally opened on the
heels of thunder, he froze and turned his
head; and for a moment his frailty was gone,
the strength returned to his blue eyes, the
power to his voice, the authority to a bearing
long since vanished with time.

"Why are you here?" Thin, high, creaking
with his chair.

"I just wanted to see if you were all right,
Father. I worry about you, you know."

"If you were worried, you wouldn't have left
me." A spasm bent him over, saliva dribbled
down his chin. He gasped, and clutched at his
chest, his lungs begging for air. "You wouldn't
have left, you sonofabitch."

"A bad way to talk about a loving son, Father."

The shadows had lowered draperies over the doorway; he could not see the man's face, but he could hear the scorn in his voice.

"You're no son of mine."

"Mother would disapprove."

"Your mother is dead, and I thank God for it."

A laugh, low and somber. "If God is listening, he's decided against you."

The old man tried to rise, but his legs failed him, his arms collapsed, and he could not lift a finger when hands came around the sides and pinned his shoulders to the chair.

"Sit still, Father, sit still. I'm only here to tell you that you will be alone this evening. I do not think my dear brother and I will be around until after midnight."

The old man coughed, and choked.

"Would you like a glass of water?"

The old man nodded.

The glass was handed to him, carefully, solicitously, and a hand held a blanket corner under his chin to catch the dripping.

Thunder, and the stormclouds forced the trees to recoil.

The glass returned to the table, the blanket was smoothed on the old man's lap, the chair turned just so in order that he may view the storm more fully.

He did not turn around when he heard the door open, and he did not make a sound when he heard the curses fill the hall. He did not care. His sons were a continual disappoint-

ment to him, as was their mother before she
passed on. And he was not so far gone that he
didn't know they were plotting against him.
Together, or as one, it didn't matter; they were
against him.

They would learn, however; they would
learn that Claude Drummond was not a man
to be crossed.

Even as he sat here, alone, forgotten, their
downfalls were plotted, were already set in
motion.

Lightning filled the window.

Claude Drummond smiled.

Lucas made an about-face so abrupt he
almost tripped over his own feet. It was
damned embarrassing, coming on Jo and
Drummond like that. But he supposed he
should have known better. He had the position, and he had the respect, but the one thing
he didn't have was the lure of good money.

He marched up the street, more angry at
himself than at Johanna, and turned into the
stationhouse. There were still quite a few
people sitting on the curved benches ranged
along the walls, waiting on Constable Newstone to listen to their complaints. They
greeted him with solemn or sullen nods, and
he counted himself lucky he was able to get
through the railing gate before someone took
his arm. Newstone was just coming out of the
storeroom with an ink pot in his hand when
Lucas stepped onto the low platform and
looked down at the desk.

"Trouble, Chief?" the policeman asked, his

voice clearly daring him to offer criticism or comment.

"Nope," he said, liking the sound of the title and wondering if he would ever get used to hearing it attached to his name. "Have you gotten word from Charlie?"

"Not a thing. If I was him, I'd find a cave and fast before I drowned."

He nodded absently, flipped through the papers and scratched the side of his neck. "You hear that wolf last night, Farley?"

"Nosir, I didn't."

"You see what happened to George Tripper and MacFarland?"

"Nosir, I didn't."

"You hear anything about Jerad Pendleton, where he might be?" He held up a hand to forestall the chorus. "If you do, get to me right away, you understand?"

"You got it, Chief."

He straightened, and stared at Newstone, at the pockmarked face and the vain attempt the sandy mustache made to cover some of the damage. He also stared at the sneering in the man's eyes, at the contempt in his stance, and with a glance to the waiting people he leaned closer and crooked a finger.

Newstone, puzzled, stepped around to his chair, pushed it aside and looked down at the papers in the chief's hand.

"Farley, it's getting late. I'm on my way over to the Drummond's to find out about Jerad."

"What the hell for?" Newstone blurted without thinking. "Jesus, Lucas, he's only a drunk."

"I'm going over to the Drummonds," he repeated without raising his voice, "and if you so much as think about leaving here and going over to see Charlotte, I will personally take both your ears off and shove them down your goddamned throat."

He smiled at the choking that overcame the smaller man, slapped him on the back, and waved for the next complainant. As he walked out the door again he knew he shouldn't have done it, knew his mood had soured because of what he'd seen at the Inn.

But it felt good. Damned good. And it helped for a moment to drive back the concern over George Tripper's boy, and the animal that had hunted in the valley the night before.

Now if he could only find Jerad and drag him back to his house safe and sound, it would at least give him something to be proud of on this already miserable first day on the job.

Ten minutes later he waited patiently on the Drummond house stoop. He had already knocked twice, was now half-turned to survey the street with faint amusement. The number of pedestrians seemed to have doubled in the past half-hour, all of them seemingly eager to taste the welcome cool air; the children fresh from their schooling played with autumn vigor, and the horses strained against their traces in their haste to find shelter from the coming storm in their stalls.

He approved without reservation, despite the impending storm's severity marked by its thunder.

The rain would be a blessing. It may not last long, they may get more than they wanted, but the respite had arrived exactly when needed.

The door opened, and he turned, the wind taking the tails of his white jacket and whipping them against his thighs. In his hand he held a narrow-brimmed grey hat. His collar was back on, his black satin tie neatly done on in a loose bow.

"Come in, Mr. Stockton, come in," a man's voice welcomed, and he stepped into the foyer, blinked against the dim light and saw Lawrence Drummond already walking awkwardly into the sittingroom on the left, the foot of his crutch loud on the oaken flooring. He followed, apologizing for the intrusion.

"No need," Lawrence said with a desultory gesture of his free hand. "No need, Mr. Stockton. We are always here to serve the capable minions of the constabulary, isn't that right, Bart?"

Bartholomew stood stolidly by the fireplace. He nodded, shook hands with Lucas and waited.

Lucas noted the unnatural turn of Lawrence's foot, found it hard to look away. "I trust you're feeling better, Larry," he said, hoping the hypocrisy did not show.

"I'll survive," was the bitter answer. "One cannot ask more than that, can one?"

"For God's sake, Lawrence," Bartholomew said in disgust. A shrug to Lucas. "Lawrence is wishing at the top of his voice he had gone with me instead of playing the hero and going

to fight the war. He'd be in one piece now if he
had, you see."

"What Lawrence wishes," Lawrence said,
"is none of your damned business."

Lucas sniffed, and studied his hat for a
moment. "And your father? Did his journey
abroad help him in any way? That is, is he
recovering?"

"As well as can be expected for a man his
age," Bartholomew said. "I'm afraid, however, that even the most prominent physicians
he consulted were unable to help him. But
thank you for asking, Lucas. And by the way,
my congratulations on your promotion."

"Yes," said Lawrence, "we're so glad we
can sleep soundly now and not worry about
the beasts of the field coming to eat out our
hearts."

"Lawrence!" Bartholomew barked. "Lucas
is a policeman, not a trapper. He does what he
can."

"I'll tell George Tripper you said that."

"Damn you, Larry, hold your foolish tongue
or go to your room!"

Lawrence could not hold back a chuckle.
"Whatever you say, Mother. Whatever you
say."

"Gentlemen, please, please," Lucas inter-
vened, wishing he could take them both by the
throat and shake them until they wept. "I
don't want to take too much of your valuable
time. But there have been two killings out in
the valley, and from the evidence I've every
reason to believe a timber wolf has decided to

visit the state early."

Lawrence fell into an armchair and scoffed. Bartholomew shrugged.

"I heard it myself last night," Lucas said. "And in view of certain matters, all I need to ask is if Jerad Pendleton has shown up for work today."

"Ah," Lawrence said. The chair's back was to the window, his face cloaked in shadow. "Ah, the lovely Miss Pendleton still hunting for her drunken uncle."

"Uncalled for, Lawrence!" Bartholomew snapped. "Mind your tongue."

"I'll mind mine if you mind yours," the shadow-voice said.

Lucas ignored the byplay. As long as he'd known them, the two brothers had never gotten along. Lawrence, the younger, had always seemed content to do as little work as possible and spend the rest of his time sniping at the world; Bartholomew, on the other hand, took his job seriously, and had surprised them all when he decided a year ago to take the Tour, alone, on the heels of his father's return.

"I assume you've not seen him since Miss Pendleton called this morning?"

"The roses are dying," Lawrence said, then stood in a single clumsy movement and clumped to the large window, leaned heavily on the crutch to watch the air darken. "The most beautiful day since I got home."

Thunder reached into the caverns of the house, and a maid scurried into the room, lighting the lamps silently, putting shadows on the walls.

When she was gone, Bartholomew cleared his throat. "Do you think him dead?"

"I don't think anything," he said. "But he's not been seen for a while, and . . ."

"I see. A nasty business." Drummond ran a finger along the mantlepiece. "Will you need hunters?"

"There are some out already. We could always use another."

"Hunters," Lawrence said without turning, "are never the hunters they seem to be."

Lucas couldn't take anymore. He thanked them for their cooperation, and left as swiftly as propriety permitted. With his hat clapped firmly on, he strode through the gate, took several paces to his right, and glanced over his shoulder. Lawrence was still in the window, an unmoving dark spectre in the deepening greylight. A shame, he thought, that such a man should have to be crippled like that; it only added fuel to his store of self-pity.

He started off again, halted in midstride and turned back.

Lawrence was gone. The trees were rasping furiously at him, and the chill of the wind penetrated his shirt to raise droplets of ice on his chest, on his arms.

A frown, and he retraced his steps until he was near the gate and staring at one of the spiked iron pickets. There, halfway down and snared by a sliver of metal, was a swatch of cloth. He leaned down to stare, took it carefully before the wind snatched it from him, and held it close to his eyes. It was dark brown, not fine material and, from the feel of it, torn off a coat.

He looked at the house, put the cloth in his pocket and headed back for the station.

Dark brown was the coat Johanna's uncle was wearing.

7

DESPITE THE ORDERED proliferation of starkly burning candles, and the hasty lighting of the green-globed gaslamps in their walled brass sconces, the Drummond house seemed filled with the darkest of midnights, a darkness that thrummed each time the thunder roared.

Lawrence watched Chief Stockton march up the street, then turned and made his clumsy way toward the staircase. His brother said nothing, and for the first time since he'd arrived home, he was grateful. He had nothing at all decent to say to that pompous jackass, nothing at all that would not provoke another debate.

Each had changed drastically since their return, each had become a stranger to the other.

And the old man didn't help, sniveling up there in his filthy stinking room, shouting threats whenever one of them passed by his door, reminding them that he was still alive, reminding them to whom the Drummond fortune still belonged.

One of these days, he thought, he was going to strangle the old bastard.

He climbed the steps in silence, fighting the pain that still lurked in his shattered foot.

He was restless. Storms always made him restless. As if they knew him, knew where he was, and were calling to him to come out. Come out, Lawrence, and play. We're your friend, come and play, come and catch the lightning.

And since those hellish days at Shiloh, since his return from the dead, the slightest suggestion that Nature was about to set loose her most potent and seductive forces against him made him feel as if he were trapped in a tomb. He had to get out. He had to leave before the walls closed around him, snared him, buried him as he had been buried under all those bodies for all those hours until a corpsman had stumbled over his outflung arm and he'd cried out, in fear, in agony, at relief that he'd been discovered.

Buried there under all the men he knew.

Buried.

All night.

Hours upon unholy hours of lying beneath dead men, feeling their slow-dripping blood land upon his face and chest, listening to the muffled thunder of cannon in the woods, listening to the screams of the dying horses, the screams of the dying men, the deep throated growling of hungry wolves who made forays of their own onto the battlefield after dark to find an easy meal.

He was not surprised.

He had seen them before.

They had come by the dozens, shadows breaking from the trees after other skirmishes, most of them immediately driven away or shot. It had been worse at the war's outset, he'd been told; now many of the scavengers were gone, leaving the dead to the buzzards and crows.

But they weren't gone that night. Not the night he lay there in such agony he could not feel a thing, while the blood dripped on his cheek and the wolf sniffed around his throat and hours became years until the corpsman uncovered him and the surgeon sent him home.

He had to get out.

The thunder was driving him crazy.

"I'm going out," Newstone declared to the room, slapping the latest complaint sheet onto an untidy pile and stuffing them into the desk drawer. He rose and stretched, rolled his head on his neck and groaned at the stiffness lodged in his shoulders. The two constables who were with him only looked at each other and shrugged. What Newstone did, direct orders or not, was his own business; Chief Stockton's wrath was something they would rather not have to face.

One day in the position, they thought in admiration, and Lucas was already in charge.

"Want to check on the Northland Avenue

gripes," Newstone said, buttoning his tunic
and slapping on his soft black cap, patting the
crown and tugging at the peaked brim.
"Seems to be more of them there than anywhere else."

No one answered. Only the thunder.

"If the Chief comes in," he called over his
shoulder, "I'll be back in an hour."

If the Chief comes in, they thought, you'd
best not be back at all.

Newstone felt their hostility, and didn't
give a damn. He'd been on this force for ten
long years, got nowhere fast, and knew by all
the gods that he should have been the one to
be voted the top position, not Lucas Stockton.
On the other hand, as long as Stockton was
out chasing ghosts and dogs, he was free to do
what he wanted. Those who worked his tour
had no guts to deny him.

He grinned, clapped and rubbed his palms
together.

The thunder cracked; lightning bounced
white lances off the cobblestones.

Hang on, Charlotte, he thought, old Farley's
coming.

Bartholomew said nothing as his brother
limped from the room. If he had his way at all,
he would say nothing to that coward for the
rest of their lives.

Instead, he remained unmoving on the
hearth and watched the leaves dart like insects past the window, watched a carriage
ride past as if Satan were on its heels,
watched his left hand begin to shake and slop

over his wrist port he had drawn for himself at the first sign of the storm.

For several minutes he smoothed the soft white leather over the backs of his hands, wincing now and then, turning them over to examine the palms, the fingers, the cut of the leather that reached up over his wrists.

A sigh.

The storm muttered, and he grimaced in an effort to keep himself from yelping.

He did not like storms.

He did not like thunder.

He did not like a single reminder of the trip he had taken. London, Brussels, Amsterdam, Paris—sinfully false cities in a sinfully false world, filled with people who shouldn't be living, people with no better purpose than to propogate themselves. Dirty people and profane people and people whose god had the voice of gold falling into a purse. Not like those he had met later on, those who lived where they wanted, those who let the wind guide them and teach them and protect them in the womb of the mountains. They had fascinated him. They had terrified him. They had, finally, permitted him to travel along with them. A lark. A bit of fluff for his exceedingly dull life . . . until the storm in the mountain pass.

He had been walking, enjoying himself, wishing he had tried harder to talk Johanna into coming with him, wishing he were a king so he could order the peasants to their deaths and the rich to his dungeons and leave only those he thought worthy of breathing.

Walking, up there in the pass, where the headlong charge of thunder utterly deafened him and the lightning blinded him and the stones loosened by the pelting cold rain slammed into his back, rolled him down the hillside and trapped him under a fallen log crawling with dead things he dared not examine, not even when he felt them working their way under his clothes.

Trapped beneath the log swarming with *things*.

Trapped.

All night.

Thinking he would surely die, wishing he would die when it was evident he would not, when it was clear he would remain there under that log, exposed to the *things*, that wriggled under his clothes, over his flesh; exposed to the *things* that came out of the trees to see what meals they could find.

Pinned.

Helpless.

Alone in the dark while the bears prowled, and the storm howled, and the wolves sniffed close around his bleeding ankles, his one free hand, his torn and naked throat because his head was pulled away by a branch pressed against his forehead. The wolves whose fetid breath made him gag, whose fur brushed over his face and made him scream so silently he thought his head would burst.

All night.

All during the storm.

Found the next day, he allowed himself to be rescued, and said nothing when the people asked him fearfully to leave.

The change in his hands was noticed when he returned to Paris, the change in himself when he took ship for home in Southampton.

He rubbed the tips of his fingers together, then headed for the coat rack by the front door, fetched down his cloak and walked into the back library where the rifles were kept in a glass-fronted cabinet affixed to the wall.

He would hunt tonight, and show Lucas Stockton what an expert could do.

Maria Andropayous cleared away the supper dishes, hustled Ned off to his room where she made sure his school books were out for his studying, then returned downstairs and looked in the study. Lucas was sitting by the window, staring out at the backyard but, she knew by the crease on his brow, not seeing a thing. As far as he was concerned, the approaching storm did not exist, nor any of the village. A hand scratched lightly at his knee, the other massaged his temple.

Her ancient head shook side to side, once, and she slipped back into the kitchen to stand at the door.

Though the sun would not set for an hour yet, night had already fallen over the Station. The wind had died, but the thunder had not, and now, at last, there were faint sparks of lightning that would arrive, she guessed, about the same time as the rain. The rain she could smell on the air, damp and heavy and filled with unseen shadows that made her decide.

There had been, for a while, the welcome
and desperate temptation to believe Lucas
when he told her she was being nothing more
than an old woman afraid of her shadow; for a
while, his soothing voice had lulled her, con-
vinced her he was right and she was wrong.

The respite, however, lasted only until he'd
returned from the stationhouse, ate his meal
in silence, said not a word to his son. She saw
then his worry, and the curious way he looked
at her—sideways, uncertain, as if lacking the
courage to ask her again what she really
meant when she told him the wolf had two
legs.

And when the interlude was over, the peace
she had almost talked into her soul, they
returned—all the fearful nightmares of her
childhood. She knew then she was not mistak-
en no matter how incredible it may seem, and
she knew there was only one way to know for
sure.

A green woolen shawl dropped lightly
around her shoulders, and she left the house,
keeping away from the study window as she
hurried as fast as her bent legs could take her
to the sprawling garden in back. Once there
she sidestepped the herbs common and exot-
ic, the vegetables she sold in the market for
extra money, until she reached a single plant
she had nurtured all the way over the Atlan-
tic, all the way to this village and her employ
with the Stocktons.

It was dark.

She could barely see.

Then a jagged crack of lightning rent the

sky above her, and in the deafening blast of thunder that followed she could see; her hands went to her mouth, but not in time to smother the moan.

The plant was wolfsbane.

The white blossom was open.

8

"BY DAMN, LUCAS!" John Webber exclaimed.
"By damn and damnation, what d'ya think I
am, a miracle worker? Good Lord in heaven,
preserve me from the idiots populating this
world." He shook his head wearily and
stomped into the living room, dropped into a
worn, straight-backed chair and stretched out
his spindly legs. Lucas followed him more
slowly after a second's hesitation, hat defer-
entially in hand, eyes avoiding the other's
glare. He did not sit when the doctor offered
him a chair. He was unaccountably nervous.

"Nice suit," Webber said with a disdainful
gesture toward the chief's white clothes. "You
practicin to be an angel?" Then he clawed in
his black waistcoat pocket and pulled out the
swatch the chief had given him. His half-
glasses slid down to the end of his nose, and
he peered, sniffed, crossed his feet at the

ankles and looked up. "Brown."

"I know that, John."

"Wool, I'd say. Bad weave, very sloppy, probably local. Suspect he got it at Carpenter's place, that hole around the corner from the bank, on Steuben. Man might as well be one for all the style he's got. His clothes suit his name, if y'know what I mean." He snorted —his version of a laugh—and shook his head again.

Lucas ran the hatbrim through his hands impatiently, and sighed when the diminutive physician held out the cloth for him to take.

"Best I can do, Lucas," Doc said. "No sign of blood. It was ripped off by that fence."

Lucas nodded. He'd come to the identical conclusions, had tried the old man in on the off-chance something had slipped past him. Nothing had. A man's coat, and Jerad had one like it, and so did half the damned village.

"You want to see the bodies again?"

"No. Once was enough, thanks."

"Good thing. Ain't had any ice today. Those boys smell to high heaven down there. I tell you, Lucas, you have no idea how difficult it is to keep a housekeeper when you have corpses in the cellar, taking up room where the potatoes ought to be. Think I'll get me a basket of lemons and cut them open down there. It's better'n nothing, believe me."

He grinned, thinking that Webber for all his complaints probably couldn't sleep at night unless there was a body in the house.

It was Webber's turn to sigh then. He took his spectacles in one hand and whirled them by the sidepiece. For a moment, in the lamp-light, he looked a hundred years old.

"Those men, I know what you mean," he said quietly, while thunder muttered outside. "I haven't seen anything so disgusting since Horace Bartlett's eldest got run over by the train. Jesus God, what a sight." He inhaled slowly, drew his legs up and replaced his glasses on his nose. "I tell you, Lucas, this is bad business, this wolf stuff."

"Barrows will get him if anyone can."

"No, that's not what I meant."

There was no fire in the grate, just a low scattering of ashes; the wind slipped down the chimney and stirred them, danced with them.

"Lucas, you know as well as I a wolf that's right don't attack a man. He's starving, yes; he's gone out of his head, yes. Otherwise," and he spread his hands wide, waiting for Lucas to nod agreement, "it isn't right."

"So we have a crazed animal, what's so odd about that?"

Webber sank deeper into his chair. Lucas could see only his thickly veined hands, the long fingers still slightly stained with dried blood under the nails. "The heart, Lucas, the heart. A wolf, like any other creature, eats what it has to. But from the stomach, the leg, anyplace where there's meat. Lucas, no animal in the world goes straight for the heart . . . and takes it."

Charlotte Notting was awakened by the thunder; she rolled over in the bed, groaning

as she stretched her arms over her head. She
was naked. The sheet was damp and clinging,
and she allowed a dreamy smile to part her
lips as she saw her second lover of the night
dressing in the corner, in the dark. It was
rather nice, actually, the way he acted so
shyly—and sure as hell not like Farley. It
made her feel special somehow, as if she were
too good to see him without his clothes. The
first time, she had taken a match to the lamp-
wick, and he'd blown it out with a snarl that
had frightened her. Then, before she could
give him a piece of her mind, he had kissed
her, apologized, told her it was his way and he
hoped she didn't mind.

She didn't.

As long as he left the gold piece on the
nightstand tray, he could run out of here buck
and shivering for all she cared.

"I didn't like it when you were gone," she
whispered, levering herself slightly upward so
the sheet would uncover the top of her ample
breasts.

"I had to go."

"Not really," she said. "And when you did,
it was for an awfully long time."

"I'm back now."

"Oh yes," she sighed. "Oh yes, you really
are."

He blew her a kiss, and she clapped her
hands together to trap it, placed a palm
against her cheek and watched as he opened
the door, turned for a look, and left her in the
dark.

Oh yes, she thought; and one of these days I'm going to be your Missus. Make no mistake about it, I'm going to have all that money and Miss Johanna Pendleton can stick to her pretty police boy.

Jeddy sat in the dark. The hot dark. Over his head the floorboards creaked when men walked through the barn; behind him spiders walked, passing over his neck, his cheek, and he could not stop crying. He could not stop whimpering, so he pressed a fist against his teeth and bit down on his knuckles.

They called his name.

They told him it was all right.

But it wasn't. It wasn't all right. There were monsters out there, far worse than the monsters that lived under the floor with him. Monsters that killed his father, that took Elijah away, and the monster had seen him, and *looked* at him, looked inside, and had shaken its great white head and walked away to kill his father.

He wasn't going out there.

He didn't care if his stomach grumbled and complained. Nothing in the world would make him leave his secret place so the monster would get him.

He would rather die.

And then he heard the scratching of the rats.

The Pendleton cottage was on High Street, a few doors west of Fox Road. A single story

high, not very wide, yet it competed well with
those high brick salt boxes that flanked it on
the street. Delia Pendleton dealt in flowers
while her husband dealt in misery; her garden was luxurious, her shrubbery rich and
green, and she spent as much time pruning
and weeding as she did in her kitchen.

Johanna sat on the front porch and watched
her now, walking through the rose beds with a
lantern in her hand, searching for blossoms
damaged by the wind. It was as if Uncle Jerad
didn't exist; and for Delia he did not, much of
the time. A pity, because the man wasn't as
bad as he appeared; shiftless, a bit on the lazy
side, and prone to bouts of infidelity he was
careful not to flaunt. Delia terrorized him,
and Johanna by her inaction felt she was
giving her aunt permission to do so.

Lucas stood in the dark of an elm and
watched her, knowing what she was thinking
because she had told him once that when she
took to the porch after dark, it was in an
attempt to discover what made her relatives
behave the way they did, and what made her
stay with them though it would not have been
difficult for her to find rooms of her own.

The lantern bobbed and dove, hovered and
moved on.

A hand rubbed the back of his neck thoughtfully, and he supposed that he could stand
here all night, just looking at her, dreaming
about her, wondering if he could compete
with Bartholomew or Lawrence, dangerously
wanting to surrender to his son's campaign to

get him a new wife.

"Good lord, Dad," the boy had said only the week before, "she's beautiful! Only a lout would let that prize get away. I'm telling you, Dad, if you don't do it one of the Drummonds will."

Lucas had stared at him open-mouthed from his chair, blinking rapidly, not believing what he'd just heard. Then the boy . . . no, the young man, had put an arm around his shoulders—the roles reversed, and he knew it—and told him that Mother was long gone, would always be alive in their memories, and how smart was it to bury yourself with her?

Not smart at all, he thought sourly, as he stepped out from under the tree and approached the walk; only I don't need my son telling me how to run my life.

Johanna jumped to her feet when she saw him, and Delia only waved a ghostly hand as she proceeded to the next rose.

"Have you heard?" Johanna said when Lucas joined her at the railing.

"Not a word, I'm afraid," he said cautiously, fingering the swatch in his jacket pocket. "I'm not worried, though."

A blush threatened to color his cheeks when she examined his face closely, shook her head and silently told him he was a liar. "It's really the boy, isn't it," she said, "You're more concerned about the boy."

The nod came before he could stop it, the nod and the guilt that he was so damned helpless to banish. "It isn't right, Jo," he said, quietly heated. "It isn't right. Charlie and I searched that place from attic to cellar, tore the barn apart, and the stable where Elijah worked. And there's nothing. Not a trace, not a print. It's as if he never was in the first place."

Johanna took his arm and leaned against him. Soft, he thought; soft and cool.

"Secret places," she suggested. "All little boys, no matter how old they are, have secret places to hide when they're scared, or when they think they've done something wrong. You know that, Lucas. You had one, and I'll bet Ned does too."

"I suppose."

She slapped his arm playfully, and for a moment the lantern stopped moving. "She thinks you're being ungentlemanly," she giggled. "A terror she is when you're not a gentleman around here."

"I can believe that," he said, keeping an eye on her aunt.

"You have to find the secret place," she said with a definite nod. "Find that, and you'll find Jeddy."

"Great," he said. "And where am I to get that kind of information? From the man in the moon?"

Johanna's dark eyebrows lifted. "Well, don't ask me, Lucas Stockton. You're the policeman. You're supposed to know these things."

In spite of himself, in spite of the image of Drummond kissing her on the street, he smiled, and looked away in embarrassment when he felt his right arm move around her waist, and felt rather than heard her grateful sigh. You're doing it, boy, he thought in abrupt panic; you're doing it, have a care.

"And what about Jerad? Did he have a place?"

"Damn right he did!" Delia said, popping up on the other side of the porch railing. Her angular face, lighted from below by the lantern, put great hollows in her sallow cheeks, canyons in her ridged brow. She wore a scalloped cloth cap that tied under her double chins, and when she thrust her face closer he could smell lavender on her breath. "You go down to the Inn, or you see that wench, Charlotte Notting." An emphatic nod, and the apparition was gone, back into the roses where her voice rose and fell in a dozen colorful curses.

Johanna began laughing, so hard she had to bury her face in Lucas's chest to keep her aunt from hearing. Lucas, on the other hand, didn't think it was funny. The old woman hated him for sins he'd never committed, preferred Drummond and his money, and her mention of Charlie's wife made him wonder why neither he nor Barrows had sent him word of their progress.

The laughing fit subsided. Johanna daubed at her eyes with a handkerchief from her sleeve, and hiccoughed. Giggled. Sniffed hard once and set her expression to something sober.

"Aunt Delia's right," she said, a hint of

melancholy in her tone.

"I've checked the Inn, so have you."

"I haven't gone to Charlotte's."

He closed his eyes briefly. "Nor I."

"You'll have to, I guess."

"No," he said. "He's not there, Johanna. Charlie's not on regular duty today. Charlotte knows that; she wouldn't take the chance."

"But surely she knows he's gone hunting for the boy."

He shrugged; she was right again, and he was stalling because he didn't want to know. Not for sure. Because if he did, if he caught Charlie's wife in bed with someone else, his affection for his subordinate might lead him to do something stupid.

Johanna moved, slipping easily between him and the railing.

"Lucas?"

He looked down, tried to appear pleasant.

"Lucas, I was wrong. It's more than just the boy. You know something, and you're not telling me." Her left hand gripped his lapel tightly. "Is it about Uncle Jerad?"

He brushed a hand through his hair, cleared his throat, and told her there was in fact something he had wished to ask her, something he decided was too outlandish to mention.

Johanna jerked a thumb over her shoulder, at her aunt combing the rose beds. "Worse than that?"

A quick laugh covered just as quickly by a cough. "I think not, now that I think about it."

"Then what?"

He pulled at his nose, tugged at the back of his hair, then shook his head and looked away. "It's something Maria told me last night."

9

FOR THE FIRST time in his twenty-four years of
hunting and tracking in and around the hills
of Oxrun Station, Charlie Notting was lost.

One moment he knew exactly where he
was, to the inch how far he was from the
Tripper farm below Pointer Hill, and the next
he didn't think he could find his ass with both
hands and a giant lantern.

It wasn't frightening, it was humiliating,
and if anyone so much as said a single word
about it, he was going to blow his stack and
turn in his badge. It was humiliating, and it
was painful.

He had spent most of the day doggedly
trailing after Barrows and his sons, listening
to the fat man snap his damned suspenders as
he bitched about Stockton, bitched about the
drought, bitched about the trees he took as a
personal affront slowing him down. It seemed

as if the entire world had decided that Donald
Barrows was going to be made a fool of, and
Barrows had decided that the world was going
to pay.

It was hell, but Charlie also listened to the
way the man expertly, uncannily read the few
tracks they had found, could tell the weight of
the animal they'd come across, its direction,
its age, all in such an off-handed manner he
had initially believed Barrows was making it
up. It was a school he'd attended with his own
father, but nothing like this; the man was
unnatural and made him feel as if he'd never
known a thing about the woods, or about
hunting.

What made him complain so much was the
complete lack of wolf tracks, or anything re-
motely resembling them.

Not a single one, not even in the field where
they found Tripper's horse.

It was Barrow's idea to begin on the far side
of the crest of Pointer Hill, down near the
quarry; if they discovered nothing of interest,
and if the Tripper boy wasn't hiding in one of
the caves there, they would sweep up, over,
and down into the valley. And if that proved
fruitless, he proposed they follow the train
tracks to the north rise and start again at the
iron mines.

They hadn't gotten that far.

Barrow's youngest took a fall at the quarry
and turned an ankle so badly Charlie thought
it was broken; the next one received a nasty
blow to his forehead when in his eagerness to
prove himself as good as his father he forgot

to duck under a low-hanging branch while running full-tilt down the slope. Two sons to take two sons back, and Barrows called a halt, broke out bread and ale, and they wasted another hour under a hickory, speculating and getting nowhere.

Then the clouds rolled in, and Barrows told him to stick around, he had an idea.

That was four hours ago.

Charlie, in his waiting, was so exhausted he fell asleep. When he awoke, disorientation unnerved him until he remembered where he was, and why. Immediately, he grabbed up his Enfield and started off on his own, calling for Barrows, receiving no answer. His head was still muzzy from the sleeping, his vision not quite as clear as it should have been, and he damned himself for not being more professional. It was the ale, of course. He never could manage ale during the day, and now it was paying him back for forgetting.

Four hours, and with the sun at last gone, the slope of the land changing every twenty paces, he had no damned idea where the hell he was.

Four hours, with thunder stalking him, the wind blinding him, the lightning finally flaring above to turn the trees to giants and the land to dead silver.

But it was only when his legs rebelled in a fierce spasm of cramping that he finally stopped, slumped against a rock and decided he would never be seen in civilization again. It infuriated him more than distressed him. He had been trying so goddamned hard to

impress the chief; he wanted so much to be
like him, and at the same time knew that
there was more than simply size the man had
in his favor. There was a bulldog stubborn-
ness, and refusal to believe that things as they
appear are always what they are.

The wind died.

Thunder like boulders rolled down on his
shoulders.

He shivered in the chill that he'd welcomed
when it first arrived, used the carbine as a
prop to haul himself wearily to his feet.

That's when he heard the first of the howling.

Donald Barrows stumbled through a briar
patch, lost his footing and fell into a depres-
sion hollowed by the departure of a boulder
twice his size. His rifle flew from his hand, his
hunting knife slipped out of its sheath, and he
wasted precious minutes scrabbling on all
fours gathering them back.

Stockton, he decided, was going to pay for
this, and pay dearly. Not a single damned sign
of bear—not to mention that stupid notion of a
wolf—for all his hard work. Stockton would
say I told you so, and pay no heed to the fact
that he'd not found a trace of wolf or bear
himself.

Besides, he thought angrily as he headed
down the slope for the fields of his own farm,
no fool wolf in God's creation does stuff like
he'd seen today. Eating like that, chewing for
the hell of it, breaking through bone and
muscle just to get to a man's heart.

Bile rose in his mouth, and he spat quickly.

Thunder and lightning collided overhead; he ducked away instinctively as if expecting a blow, cursed loudly just to hear the sound of his voice as he started moving again.

Worse and worse; now that jackass kid Notting was nowhere to be found. Not that he blamed him for not sticking around. If he had any brains at all—which he sincerely doubted —given the chance he was probably off to home, snuggling with his young wife, taking her skirts, taking her blouse. There was no question Charlotte was a ripe one, and no question but that Barrows would someday find out exactly how ripe she was.

What Charlie didn't know was that beneath all that cotton, beneath all them petticoats, was a highway well traveled by anyone who knew the road.

The hell with him, then.

Barrows would take the wolf, bear, whatever the hell it was, and nail it proper to Stockton's goddamn door, make that idiot Charlie look the proper fool and get his just reward when Stockton put Notting on the Mainland Road coach to protect the women and the mail.

He wished he'd thought to bring a lantern.

A pause to catch his breath, and he heard it.

Footsteps coming fast behind him.

He turned with Charlie's name harsh and mocking on his lips, and saw nothing.

The woods were as empty as the sudden hollow in his stomach.

Trees in writhing dark array, the foliage

laughing like ghosts above him, the infrequent flashes of lightning to show him the empty path.

But he heard them, damnit, they were still there, and he felt no shame in turning around and starting to walk. Faster. At a trot. Not knowing why he did, only knowing it wasn't Charlie or any of his sons coming at him from behind; it was someone he didn't want to know, not out here in the dark.

The trees fell away.

He was in the back pasture on George Tripper's farm.

Ahead of him a flat-topped boulder rose a full ten feet above the ground, black against black until, with a suddenness that made him blink, the wind died. The thunder died. The clouds began to part and show him the full moon.

Mist rose in pale strands from the furrows, grey writhing serpents that coiled slowly around his ankles; Pointer Hill behind him, a solid ebony wall whose weight pressed hard against him, made him take a cautious step forward; the Spencer in his hand, swiftly up to his chest, hammer back, finger curled around the trigger while he circled the rock.

That was it, Donald, he told himself gleefully.

Thirty years of hunting had honed an edge to his instincts, had given him a nose for game and a sense of impending triumph. The earth smelled damp, the air heavy with rain not yet fallen. He moved sideways, silently, until the boulder was between him and the bulk of the hill. Nothing huddled at the base, nothing loping across the field, and in the far comforting distance he could see the lights of his house.

The footsteps again, running so fast he had the rifle to his shoulder and his eye on the sight before they came to a halt. A dead halt. A *hissing* of passing air. A vacuum that made him shake his head to bring back sound.

Any sound.

It did.

A *scratching* on the far side of the boulder, nails against stone. Something climbing; something large.

Barrows nodded and squared his feet, set his shoulders. He was ready, and Stockton was about to proclaim him a hero. He moved carefully away . . . until the boulder was full in sight, the moon lifting directly behind it. A huge pocked moon framed by the passage of black clouds.

scratching

Barrows swallowed, aimed, held his breath.

He almost fired reflexively when the lank figure of a man rose atop the boulder. A tall man. Deep black against the moon. His hands were in fists, his arms lifted to the sky, and though Barrows could not see his face, he knew he had been seen.

Then his vision sharpened, and he saw who it was.

"Well, what the hell . . . ?" he said, his amazement forcing a hand to rub his face to be sure he was right. He lowered his weapon, leaned on it like a cane. "What the bloody hell are *you* doing out here?"

From the black of the black figure where the head should have been, he spotted a puzzling glint of color, a blinking, a widening until he saw two slanted eyes gleaming darkbright amber.

"Hey, look, you wanna come down now? It ain't safe up there, y'know? My God, man—"

The figure of the man turned his head to the clouds and from his open mouth came the first of the howling.

Barrows dropped his rifle, felt his knees begin to give.

"Hey, what the hell are you—"

A baying while the figure began to writhe without moving, began to shimmer without reflecting, began to transform itself from shadow black to a deadly flat white.

The baying, the howling, a frenzied call of demonic triumph.

It filled Barrow's ears until he dropped to the ground, not believing what he heard, not believing what he saw, looking up despite his terror and seeing the nightbeast on the rock.

A wolf.

Huge, white, with staring amber eyes; huge, swaying, its claws already out and *scratching* slowly against stone; huge, panting, its fangs slicing the moon's surface when its head lifted again to bay.

Barrows scrambled for the rifle.

The wolf swung its head around.

Barrows couldn't find the trigger.

It licked its lips.

And sprang.

Farley Newstone walked briskly up Northland, glowering at his shadow, angry at himself for risking Stockton's wrath by leaving despite orders. And what did he have to show for it? Nothing. At least, nothing tangible he could take back to his dreams.

He had arrived at the house unannounced as usual, but to his complete amazement, Charlotte had not been pleased to see him. She was clearly on the verge of asking him to leave, and he'd been forced to show her the contents of his purse.

Friendly enough, then, but something less than enthusiastic.

The little whore, in fact, had just about tossed him out the door once he'd finished dressing. And the way things were going now, he thought sourly, Lucas would be waiting for him at the station, ready to make good his promise and tear off his ears.

His pace quickened past the wooded lot between the Crenshaws and the Drummonds. The wind stirred, the moon high and bloated, and he knew there'd be rain before midnight had passed. A good thing too, he thought, idly scanning the silvered trees; people would get their tempers back, making his job a lot simpler.

He smelled the blood before he saw the body—acrid, wrinkling his nose, forcing him to cover his mouth with a palm while he peered into the grey shadows . . . and saw the mangled leg sticking out from beneath a shrub.

Warily, one hand on his nightstick while he swallowed hard and fast, he stepped into the underbrush, jumping when thunder began rumbling again.

Then lightning ripped across the moon, and he saw with a gasp what was left of Jerad Pendleton.

Charlie Notting gripped the slender bole of a sapling maple and gaped. War within him raged against what he had just seen, and reason shrieked that his getting lost on famil-iar ground had driven him mad.

But he *had* seen it.

He had seen the man on top of the boulder, had seen him raise his fists to heaven and . . . *change*. It was no trick of the moonlight, no distortion from the lightning; the man had changed to a monstrous demon, a hideous white wolf that had leapt off the boulder just as Charlie had grabbed the tree.

The baying was horrid.

The single, short-lived scream made him slump to the ground, shivering, sobbing, while he heard the nightbeast eating.

An hour, and when his head lifted he knew he was alone.

Ten minutes, and he dried his face with a sleeve, pulled himself to his feet and stum-bled out of the woods. He did not want to see the body, though he knew who it must be; he wanted a horse, and right away, and broke into a shambling panicked run straight for George Tripper's barn.

Lucas wouldn't believe him.

Charlie would kill him if he didn't.

10

THE AIR CONTINUED cool, and August almost
seemed dead.

The wind lurked overhead, shaking a
branch, dropping a shower of twigs and
leaves, darting every so often into the street to
push at a dust devil and set it in motion. A
horse's hooves echoed. Carriage wheels rolled
over the cobblestones like caissons.

It was late, long past ten, yet a fair number
of pedestrians and riders were reluctant to
surrender their beguilement by the temperature's change. They knew it wouldn't last, and
they wanted some comfort from it.

Lucas and Johanna left the porch, and the
garden, to Aunt Delia's continued fussing,
and strolled around the near corner, heading
for Chancellor Avenue. She kept her hand on
his arm, her head tilted slightly in his direction, waiting for his story. Instead, as though
stalling while he gathered his thoughts, he

spoke about his day, the horrid things he had seen, the way the villagers were overreacting to the promise of simple rain. It wasn't natural, he believed; they were afraid of whatever it was that had killed out in the valley, and he wasn't at all sure he could offer them adequate comfort.

"Like you and Jerad," he said morosely. "Ever since I received the promotion, I just can't seem to do anything right. It's enough to drive a man crazy. This place isn't all that big, yet I can't seem to find one lousy man, one simple missing drunk sleeping it off somewhere."

"You're feeling sorry for yourself," she chided.

He thought to argue, changed his mind and nodded. "Yes, I suppose I am. But can you blame me? My god, I'm so frustrated I could chew nails and spit rust."

And he remembered Bartholomew Drummond, and the scene at the Inn.

"None of this is your fault, you know."

"Of course I know that," he snapped. "I'm not that much of a fool. But it is my responsibility to clear things up."

"Well, what more do you have to do, Lucas?" she said with a frown. "You have hunters out there in the woods, you have men with guns on the street . . . good heavens, you're not God, you know. You can't be everywhere at once."

He bridled at the well-intended scolding, more so because he knew what she said was true, and could not shake the feeling he had missed something vital. He rubbed a hard hand over his face, and groaned, shook his head.

"You, Lucas Stockton, are impossible," she declared, reading his thoughts and squeezing his arm. "It's a wonder Maria hasn't locked you in the cellar."

Her laugh, then, was light as her hair fanned over her face, was swept away and streamed behind her, and he was glad she did not affect the high-brimmed bonnets ladies of fashion seemed to like; her eyes were too lovely and expressive, her mouth too full to hide behind lace. And he was just as glad she did not wear gloves, so he could feel the strength as well as the warmth of her hand on his arm.

"Yes," she said with a decisive nod, "you are impossible."

He couldn't help agreeing, covered her hand with his as he directed his gaze straight ahead to the Avenue. The late coach from Harley rumbled past, in and out of shadow, post lanterns swinging, the driver pointing his long whip up at the sky.

She cleared her throat lightly and glanced up at him, looked away. "Bart proposed to me this afternoon," she whispered.

He nodded despite the lurch of his heart. "I thought as much. I saw you. On the street after your dining."

"Do you care?" she asked boldly.

He stopped, turned her to face him. "Damnit, yes."

A mischievous grin made her ten years

younger. "How much do you care?"

"I care enough to match the offer," he said, groaned inwardly at his impulsiveness and swore he would have a long talk with his son.

"I shall consider it," she answered primly, and started them walking again. "For now, however, there are matters to attend to. Tell me about Maria."

He sputtered helplessly at the abrupt change of subject, wondering if he'd been accepted or put off, decided he wouldn't know until someone finally told him. So he talked, then, of Maria and her dark mutterings, and the longer he spoke the more foolish he felt, forcing a harsh laugh every few steps to prove to her that he of all people was certainly not influenced by galloping superstition.

"Maybe you should be," she said.

"What? Johanna, you must be joking."

"No, I'm not," she said somberly. A few short paces of contemplative silence before she spoke again. "Lucas, you once told me that it is very important to your job that you never ignore what anyone tells you. That you can always find something to use in what people say."

"Well . . . yes," he said doubtfully, "I do try, though it's deuced hard sometimes. But what does that—"

"Well, I'm trying to do the same, don't you see? I've heard all you've said and know all you're concerned about, and I'm not saying that you're doing a bad job—Lord, no, Lucas—but you're leaving something out, something that makes it clear to me you think Maria knows something you should."

"She knows nothing," he insisted heatedly. "She's just an old woman from some strange people who don't even have a country to call their own. Wanderers. Fortune-tellers. That's all she is." But he remembered vividly what John Webber had said, and he finally wondered aloud if there could possibly be a connection.

They reached the corner and stopped. To their left a scruffy lamplighter was growling to himself as he climbed a far post to rekindle a wick blown out by the wind before too much gas escaped; to their right a group of men in stove-pipes and grey cut-aways were leaving the Inn, laughing, staggering, one pinwheeling into the street and tossing his hat high into the air.

Her lower lip drew in between her teeth, and she hesitated yet again. "I know you well, Lucas," she finally said. "Better than you think."

His smile was at last genuine. "Yes, so I've gathered."

She nudged him with an elbow. "Then it seems to me, Mr. Stockton, that you are more shaken by Maria's talk than you want to admit."

The party from the Inn swept past them then, loudly, singing, only barely modifying their exhuberance when they recognized the chief. Their efforts to remain silent were more noisy than their singing.

Across the street and down the facing road he could see a man running in his direction.

"Jo," he said at last, giving vent to the fears that had stalked him throughout the afternoon, "you . . . you are recently arrived here. I have lived in Oxrun Station all my life, and things . . . I don't know quite how to put it, but things happen here that seldom happen in the outside world. All our new sciences, all our learning, cannot account for them. Yet they happen nevertheless. People die because of them. People vanish as if they had never existed at all. I've done my reading, Jo. I have listened to the talk. I know this to be true."

The man, nearer, began waving his arms in a frenzied semiphore. Lucas peered through the shadows and recognized Farley Newstone.

"Then you must tell me what you think," she insisted, tugging on his arm. "My uncle—"

The constable began shouting, and Lucas carefully disengaged her hand to turn and face him, a demand at his lips to know why the man had deliberately left the station against his express orders. Newstone, however, was babbling by the time he raced awkwardly across the Avenue, his face drawn and his eyes wide. It took no longer than a half-minute of listening, however, before Lucas curtly ordered Johanna back to the house and took the terrified man's arm, led him back the way he'd come.

Johanna vacillated between sudden fear for her uncle, and obeying Lucas's wishes. It took less than a second to decide that she would learn more by tagging along than hiding behind her aunt. Lucas saw her, and scowled, but continued on at a brisk pace, until he reached the wooded lot and waved both of them back.

The moon was gone, the wind rising.

He reached into his jacket pocket and pulled out a packet of matches, slid open the box and struck one, cupping the flame with his palms. The light was dim, but he could see clearly enough, and he spun away from the mangled body, from the torn throat, from the bloody hand that reached skyward from its bed of dead leaves, pleading for mercy.

He staggered out to the pavement, where Newstone was mopping his face frantically, and Johanna was twisting her hands at her waist.

"Farley," he said brusquely, "get to the station, bring three men back, and have someone get to John Webber."

Newstone rushed off without argument; Johanna saw the look on the chief's face and made to step around him.

"No," he said gently, voice filled with condolence.

"Oh God . . . no," she whispered, and took to his arms while he stared unblinkingly up the street. At the Drummond house. At the spiked fence, where he'd found the piece of cloth.

When Newstone returned, Lucas directed that no one except the doctor be permitted in the wood, then brought Johanna back to the station where he settled her in the office, pulled the gift bottle from his desk and poured them both a dram. She was shaken. The glass trembled in her hand.

"Why?" she asked. "What did he ever do?"

"I don't know," Lucas answered. "I wish I did, but I just don't know."

"Lucas, what is it?" she pleaded, her eyes brimming tears. "What is it?"

Whatever he would have said died in his throat. At that moment, loud excited voices were suddenly raised in the front room, and he stomped to the door, threw it open and bellowed for silence. Then Charlie Notting broke away from a crowd of fellow officers and staggered toward him, his uniform atangle, his hair plastered with mud and dried grass. He pointed behind him, put a hand to his chest and pushed by into the office, barely noting Johanna who had jumped to her feet.

Lucas followed, put the young man into his own chair and stood over him. There was only a single lamp glowing in the room. It might as well have been pitch dark.

"I found him," Charlie finally gasped. "The boy, I've found the boy."

Lucas grinned and looked to heaven. "Thank the Lord something is going right tonight!"

Charlie shook his head; a shiny black beetle fell from his beard and dove between the floorboards. Lucas poured him a brandy as well, forced him to drink it all down before attempting to speak again. Then without turning around asked Johanna to go out front, to see to the boy and bring him back here. She agreed readily.

After a hand wiped his mouth, combed through his beard, Charlie slumped back and stared at the chief. His youth was gone; his eyes were sunk deeply into his face, and he could not stop himself from shaking his head.

"Barrows is dead," he said at last.

Lucas turned up the lamp; it did no good.

"I saw what killed him."

"The wolf," Lucas said, hoping against the cold that had settled in his stomach that he was right; that it was, in fact, no more than that.

"Jesus," said Charlie, "I only wish it was!"

11

THE HOUSE WAS dark, steeped with the chill of
the passing storm. Boards creaked, shadows
danced obscenely in the windows, and a faint
soughing drifting in the mouth of the sitting
room hearth.

At the head of the staircase a figure moved.
Stiffly, though less painfully than before. One
gnarled hand pressed to the wall for balance,
the other clutching a shawl closed about the
neck as if to ward off the odd summer cold.
Claude Drummond, his wasted face contorted
with rage, cocked his head and listened . . .
and heard nothing.

Alone, then.

He was still alone.

A funereal cackle broke from his lips, and
he continued down the hall. Searching, testing the air for unwanted disturbance, peering
into the corners and poking at the dark. The
rooms were empty; his sons were gone. And

though he wanted desperately to end it now,
his plans would not permit it. He was trapped
by them, because they were his and he had
never in his life changed a plan once begun.

Soon, he promised himself; soon it would be
all over. Soon he would have his revenge on
those who had tried to take what was rightful-
ly his away.

They would be surprised, and perhaps they
would be shocked, and perhaps they would
even attempt to take his life. And he cackled
again, almost wishing they would. In fact, he
thought as he returned to his room, he might
welcome the chance to get them face to face.

Poetic justice, with just a touch of horror
thrown in for good measure.

The house was dark, not a single light show-
ing save for a tiny candle at the bedside.
Charlotte sat on the edge of her bed and
brushed her golden hair down over her soft
round shoulders. The candlelight burnished
it, released the sparks trapped within, and she
hummed merrily to herself all the songs she
knew from the variety halls she'd been taken
to before she'd married that dunce, Charlie.

She was, in a word, happy.

She had made up her mind—tomorrow she
would put on her best dress, her best bonnet,
carry her parasol over her shoulder, and walk
boldly to the house where her future lay.
Charlie would question her, and she would
tell him the truth—that she married him only
because she thought he'd make good his
promise and take her to Boston. He hadn't. He

had fallen under the spell of that ugly giant, Lucas Stockton, and it was clear he would never leave the Station at all.

She, on the other hand, would.

With a Drummond at her side she would bid farewell to this miserable little place and find her rightful position in Boston's society.

And if Drummond refused her, she would tell all; she would fill the Station's ears with everything she knew, and Drummond would spend the rest of his life in prison.

She was, at last, completely in charge.

Nothing was going to stop Charlotte Notting now.

The house was dark, the only lights glowing were in the kitchen where two gas lamps flickering dimly on the walls, and one hanging from a braided brass chain over the table. Lucas sat at the table's head, Johanna on his right, Charlie on his left, Maria directly opposite. Ned had been rousted from his bed and was in the front room with Jeddy Tripper, doing his best to make the grim-faced lad smile, or cry, utter any sound at all.

From the moment Jo had brought him into the office, he had not spoken a word.

That was when Lucas said, "It's time to see Maria."

Their faces were bathed in shadow as the flames swayed in their amber chimneys, none more than the old woman whose hair, for the first time since Lucas had known her, was loose and unbraided, hanging in a thin white curtain down around her berobed shoulders.

He could see nothing of her eyes except deep black sockets, saw no movement except an occasional twitch of her hands clasped on the table.

After arriving from the stationhouse and seeing Ned to the boy, they listened patiently as Charlie described in sobbing fits and starts what he had seen in the valley. No one questioned him; no one expressed a single word of disbelief. They listened while he gulped at the brandy Lucas poured with a free hand, watched as his face alternately flushed and paled, held their tongues when he broke down once and sobbed his terror.

And just as he finished, the rain began.

A faint scratching at the kitchen window's pane, unsure, almost timorous, before it gathered its courage and slammed in great sheets against the side of the house. It was loud, and visible only when lightning turned it to quicksilver, thunder banished it to ebony.

One lamp flared, and winked out.

Johanna rose to relight it, and took the opportunity to look into the front room. Ned, his nightshirt billowing around his scrawny legs, had Jeddy on his lap and was telling him a story. The boy stared open-mouthed into his face, one arm around his neck, the other limp in his lap. Ned looked up and gave Johanna a reassuring smile without missing a word. His eyes told her it wouldn't be long before Jeddy would be talking.

Lucas, jacket off and shirt unbuttoned at the collar, took a deep breath when Charlie was done, reached out and gripped the man's wrist and held it, shook the arm once in understanding, and nodded when Charlie finally put down his glass. Then he looked to Maria Andropayous.

"I need to know," he said tonelessly. "If you have anything to give me, I need to know."

A wisp of white drifted across her face, hung there like a spider's web in front of her black, demanding eyes. He could feel her gaze measuring him, weighing him, boring into his skull to root at his mind.

"Do you?" she asked, her voice almost angry, her accent heavy and rolling. "Do you really need to know what I know, in here?" And she thumped a fist against her frail chest.

He did not hesitate; he nodded.

"Be sure, Lucas Stockton. Be sure in your heart you want to know what I know."

He looked to Jo, to Charlie, and finally back to the woman who had kept him sane and his son healthy all these years.

"I must know," he said firmly. "I must stop the dying."

She sighed soundlessly.

A minute passed.

Another.

Johanna chewed fitfully at her lower lip; Charlie sucked at his.

Five minutes, ten, before her right hand slipped off the table and into her lap. When it returned the hand was closed, and she stretched out her arm, pulled back the sleeve of her robe. They leaned forward as one, eyes on the boney fingers, the translucent flesh, the collapsing veins that trailed past her wrist across her arm. Then she turned the hand over and let her fingers fall open.

A blossom, white and fragrant, sat on her palm.

"Wolfsbane," she said, startling them all with the harshness of her voice.

"It's . . . it's beautiful," Johanna whispered.

Maria shook her head emphatically. "It is the devil's eye, my child, and beautiful only in the way a deadly snake is before it strikes."

Charlie leaned away as if to deny its existence. His eyes were wide, his chest rising and falling while he tried to catch a breath.

"What does it mean, old woman?" Lucas said quietly, intently. "What does it have to do with . . . with Jerad Pendleton, and the others, with what Charlie here told us?"

It was obvious the old woman was struggling with sorrow; not a grieving sorrow, but one that afflicts those who see the onset of unavoidable death. A death she had witnessed too many times before, one she had prayed never to have to face again.

"It is a sign," she said.

Lucas tried to smile. "Like the tea leaves?" And he wished immediately he had not spoken.

Maria glared at him so harshly he jerked away as if from a stinging blow, and the ancient hand closed swiftly over the blossom. The fingers tensed, then crushed it, and the room was suddenly flooded with a rotting-corpse stench that made them all gasp and cover their mouths and noses. Lucas buried his watering eyes in the crook of his elbow. Johanna coughed loudly. Charlie staggered to his feet and flung open the back door; rain splattered at them over the threshold while he retched and choked.

When the old woman opened her hand a second time, she stared directly at Lucas and gave him a mirthless smile. He could not believe his eyes—the flower was whole, and the stench was driven from the room by the wind.

Charlie returned to his seat, shivering so much that Johanna put an arm around his shoulders and rocked him absently, not seeing the gratitude that washed over his face.

"It is wolfsbane," Maria said again, looking only at Lucas. "It is a flower found in many parts of the world, a very special flower that I have brought with me." She poked a finger at it, drew away as if seared by some invisible flame. "It opens only at night, and only when there is something to tell."

"Tell what?" he said, more respectfully now. "What does it tell you, Maria?" She stared at him without responding, until he remembered what she had seen in the tea leaves the night before. "The wolf walks on two legs, is that it? Some sort of killing beast?"

She nodded.

"But none do," Johanna protested mildly.

"Child," Maria said kindly and patiently, "I am an old woman. But I am not so old that I lose what I have in my mind." Her hair drifted again across her face, and she brushed it away slowly, as though parting a veil. "I have come to this country like others like me . . . to get away from those who fear us and would do us harm."

"Afraid of you?" Charlie said incredulously, looking from Lucas to Johanna in hopes they would laugh. "Maria, who . . . why would anyone possibly be afraid of you?"

She sat back in her chair, let the blossom fall into the circle of light in the center of the table. Her face was hidden by shadows that parted and closed, climbed and fell away, and none of them could look at her for long without shivering.

"They fear my people, they fear me," she said, not without a trace of long-suffered melancholy, "because I know things. Not like you find in your books, not in your churches, not in your schools. I know different things. My people know different things. Things of this world and not of this world that none of you can possibly imagine, and things you never want to imagine. Things that would keep you from your sleep for the rest of your life. Things no man should ever have to know."

Her voice had strengthened, though it had not lost its age, and they all drew closer to the table, as if trying to escape the reach of the shadows behind them.

The rain fell; thunder muttered.

"And one of the things I know," she said, "is this—that in this village a creature walks, Lucas Stockton. Not a man who kills like you have imagined, and not a wolf strayed from his home and seeking only food. A creature such as one you have never seen before in your life."

"Maria—"

"Be still, and *listen!*"

After a moment of shifting, the silence was complete.

They could hear in the front room Ned telling his story.

They could hear in the kitchen the pull of their breathing.

And finally, through the insistent drumming of the rain, the distant cannonade of thunder, they all heard it.

The baying.

The shattering of the night of a full-throated voice that made Jeddy bury his face in Ned's side, had Johanna scrambling for Lucas's hand, had Charlie cover his face and whimper.

A baying, a howling, the dark cry of the moon.

Lucas glanced at his hands, saw them clenched so tightly the knuckles were bled white.

Maria leaned her face back into the light, looked straight at him and pointed.

"A wolf on two legs," she repeated. "And not a wolf."

He showed her his puzzlement.

She sighed and closed her eyes, her lips moved in voiceless prayer. When she stopped, she reached out and took hold of the blossom between two fingers and held it up.

"When the wolfsbane blooms, and the moon

is full, there walks about the land a man under a curse." And again she looked directly at Lucas.

The howling seemed nearer.

Unearthly.

A fiend.

"Lucas Stockton," she whispered, "what you hear now is that man. What you hear is a werewolf."

12

GOD GO WITH you, Lucas Stockton . . . but the Devil walks tonight.

The shiny black umbrella was large enough to protect the three of them from the savage downpour. They hastened along the deserted street while rain gouted from the sky, smashed against the cobblestones and fountained up again. Tendrils of anxious mist wove themselves to tangles beneath hedges, in the gutters. Foliage sagged, groaning branches were beaten and whipped by the wind. A loose shutter slammed against the side of a house.

There was no sense talking; all they could hear was the storm.

The Devil walks.

Lucas felt the cold eating its way into his bones, far worse than it should have been this time of the year, and he braced himself against it as if he were walking through December. Though Johanna was trembling in the circle of his arm, and Jeddy in hers, he could feel nothing; all his senses were overrun by Maria's solemn voice explaining what manner of beast he was dealing with now, what midnight creature had stalked into the village.

He will change at the full moon, and change at will; he will feed for his hunger, he will kill for his rage.

A terrible thing, Johanna had said; *what torment he must be suffering, what hell he must live in.*

Only, Maria told her, *if he does not wish it; there are some who* seek *the bite of the werewolf, some who want to run in the shadow of Satan.*

He believed it. He had seen the way Elijah had been savaged, seen the way poor Jerad had been taken.

When Maria was done, no balm for their fear, there had been no doubts, and no questions; too many times he had heard the nighttime stories that in other places would have been dismissed as the ravings of a lunatic, the imagination of a tale told of dark faeries. Lucas knew better. He instinctively knew there were forces about him which were beyond the rationale of scholarly books and university lectures.

He knew.

And he believed.

And he listened through the rain for the sound of something following, listened for the baying.

You may carry the gun, yes, but you need silver, not lead or iron.

At Delia Pendleton's cottage they huddled under the protection of the porch roof and he asked again if Johanna were sure she wanted to do this.

"I can't very well stay with you, now can I?" she said with a brave brief smile. "Besides, Jedadiah—"

"Jeddy!" the boy insisted, lower lip protruding angrily.

She tousled his hair and shrugged. "All right . . . Jeddy. He needs us, Lucas. Delia will scrub him up, and I'll tend to his cuts and scratches. We'll be fine. We'll . . . be fine."

"Sure," Jeddy said. "I'll watch them, Chief. Don't you worry, I'll watch them."

He was reluctant to leave, and knew that he must. Quickly, then, before the parting became impossible, he kissed Johanna's cheek and held her close for her warmth, grabbed the boy's thin shoulders and held them a moment before lifting his longcoat's collar high and stepping back into the rain.

Water drummed deafeningly on the umbrella.

Puddles and lakes formed along the pavement.

I gotta go back, Chief. Charlotte's alone.

He saw in the dark the outlines of homes, trees, hedges, low walls. Gleaming when distant lightning gave the air a silver coating, shifting when their shadows eased out to ensnare him.

I can take care of myself, don't worry. I

saw that thing, remember, and I can run like hell if I have to.

A shudder quite apart from the chills walked his spine; Charlie had gone, had disappeared headlong into the storm as soon as Maria had finished her warning. Lucas had tried to stop him, but the young man would not be deterred from rushing to his wife's side, and he had almost wept when the door closed behind him.

He turned the corner onto Devon Street, his eyes narrowed as he glanced up and down Chancellor Avenue. The globes of the ornate streetlamps were shimmering as if drowned in a vast obsidian lake, the water running beneath them in pale gold rivulets.

There was no one abroad, and though he didn't like the feeling, he was somehow glad that he had been left alone.

But when he turned to head home, a shadow moved with him, contrary to the wind.

A half-dozen hurried paces, and he saw it up ahead, faltered and waved a hand as though brushing away the rain.

At first he was sure it was nothing but his imagination, a remnant of the waking nightmare he felt after listening to his housekeeper. Then it moved again, there in the middle of the street at the far end of the block. It waited between two faint sprays of lamplight, but Lucas could see at once it was no ordinary shadow.

It was white, and from its proud high-slung head sparked two slanted orbs of darkbright amber.

His throat dried instantly though he tried hard to swallow; his heart swelled in his chest and made his breathing shallow. A gust of wind lashed pellets of water into his eyes; he blinked rapidly to clear them . . . and the white creature moved into the dim swaying glow.

Even at the distance which separated them, he knew it was immense. Charlie was right in every respect—it was white, and it was larger than any wolf or dog he'd ever seen, and its whiplike tail snapped at the air behind it.

The Devil walks tonight

He took one step forward, and it saw him.

Lucas knew it was watching, despite the fact that its head did not move, nor did its mouth open.

It was watching him.

It was waiting.

He took another step toward the house, a man gingerly testing the thickness of ice, and held his breath.

It was waiting.

A glance behind him, the rain falling from his umbrella in glittering strands, the wind mocking him from its laughing place under the eaves.

Another step, and he found a rhythm—a striding so slow he was barely able to keep his balance.

And still it watched him.

Its fur thick, its ears pricked high, standing on powerful legs that seemed poised to spring.

Lucas kept his gaze steadily on it, blinking only when a dark trunk passed between them,

when the wind spat in his eyes, when a way-
ward leaf swirled out of the dark like a bat on
the hunt. His boot heels struck the brick
pavement loudly, too loudly, and because of
the storm he could hear no echoes.

He was ten feet from the house when the
night-beast shifted its front paws to face him
more directly. He froze, bit hard on the inside
of his cheek and welcomed the pain, his grip
on the umbrella's pole cramping his fingers
until he forced himself to loosen his grip.

The head lifted, and its fur rippled in waves
from the thick mane behind its ears to the
plume of its slow-lashing tail.

It began to walk toward him.

The rain fell on its back, and slid off as if
striking glass.

Lucas ordered himself to move again, and
felt his legs pressing along the hedge, twigs
snapping at him damply, water dripping onto
his trousers, into his low boots.

Water splashed silently away from its paws;
its claws scraped on stone.

A trickle of ice slipped beneath Lucas's
collar, made him inhale, hissing between
tightly clenched teeth.

Its eyes sparked.

It snarled.

Its upper lip pulled back to reveal sabre
fangs, and the snarl from its chest rumbled in
tune with the thunder.

Dark bright amber eyes narrowed and
flared.

He wasn't going to make it. It would take
three running strides to reach the gate-breach

in the hedge, five or six more to reach the porch, and the safety of the door. By that time the creature would be on his back, and tearing. He wasn't going to make it, and he wasn't surprised.

A look, then, and the front windows were dark, down the side at the back the kitchen window glowing; Maria was still up, waiting for him and praying, and he was within shouting distance, waiting to die.

Patient.

Stalking.

The snarl to a low growl.

He eased forward again, the trees passing like the bars of a cage, the hedge husking, the house looming so near he felt he could stretch out a hand and touch the door's knocker. A pebble snapped from under his sole; a sodden leaf caused him a momentary slip that clamped the breath in his lungs until he knew he wouldn't fall.

Out of the street, onto the pavement.

The head lowered until its muzzle was less than an inch above the ground; the teeth were bared fully; the eyes fixed on his, and would not release him.

He almost stumbled when the hedge fell away, found himself backing toward the porch, furling the umbrella into a makeshift sword.

The wolf reached the hedge and disappeared into it.

A heel kicked against the steps, and Lucas climbed them backwards, still not daring to run, still not able to find the voice that would call Maria to the door. He reached behind him, and the door was locked. His eyes closed briefly. Grating sand filled his mouth.

The wolf stepped around the hedge.

And lunged without warning.

Lucas cried out, and slashed at the ravening beast with the broadside of the umbrella as he fell against the door, shouting at the top of his newly found voice. The metal tip of the fragile, useless weapon grazed the creature's head, the side thudded against its neck, and its leap was deflected, but only at the cost of the umbrella itself, which snapped in half with a gunshot crack, and sent a hundred stinging lances along the length of Lucas's arm.

The wolf landed neatly by the railing, and spun around while Lucas kicked back at the door, calling for Ned, for Maria; it watched him, almost smiling; white on the darkened porch, amber floating in the air.

Behind him, Lucas heard muffled footsteps.

"Ned, for god's sake!" he shouted.

The wolf leaned back, virtually sitting on its haunches, and raised its head.

And howled.

The cry made Lucas clamp his hands to his ears to stifle the sudden explosion of pain.

Howling.

His knees gave way, and he fell to the flooring, scrabbled at the door, weeping now and begging.

Howling.

And . . . silence.

Blinking his vision clear, he saw the wolf

bare its fangs again, saw the glint of its ra-
zored claws, saw it gather itself to leap.

It growled in a ravenous frenzy, and leapt
. . . just as the door swung open and spilled
Lucas over the threshold.

The wolf slammed against the wall, whirled
to spring again, but Maria was there beside
Ned, and as Lucas ducked to absorb the creature's blow on his back, he saw her arm shoot
forward, saw something flash over his head
. . . and heard the beast scream in unearthly
agony.

The blow never came, and he hauled himself to his feet. Staggering back into his son's
steadying arms while the wolf leapt over the
railing and vanished in a bound into the rain.

Maria turned away.

On the porch, rolling side to side, Lucas saw
the candlestick Madeleine had given him on
their wedding day; an unadorned candlestick
made entirely of silver.

13

WHEN THE STATIONHOUSE doors blew inward
for the second time in an hour, Constable
Farley Newstone came to a decision. He was
alone in the front room when he yelled his
disgust at the storm, alone when he bulled
through the railing gate and slammed the
doors closed, alone when he swiped at the rain
on his trousers and muttered imprecations
against the universe, Oxrun Station, and par-
ticularly Lucas Stockton.

He had had it.

First Charlotte had treated him as if he
were a perfect stranger likeable only for his
money, then poor Jerad all torn up like that in
the brush, and then Stockton putting him on
the desk for the night. All by himself. With
orders to come running as soon as he heard
the wolf.

Sure. Just like that he was going to run out
in the storm, run all the way to Stockton's

place, and knock sweet as you please on the door. Sir, the wolf is about, sir. Just following orders.

Damn!

He stomped back to the desk, grabbed his coat from the back of his chair, and shrugged into it.

The hell with him. The hell with them all. Twice in the last four months his cousin in Boston had written to ask him if he wanted a job. It wasn't police work; it was working with a private firm specializing in guarding the rich. It may be boring, but it paid better than this, and it didn't include wolves running around tearing out your heart.

The hell with them. The hell with them all.

He clapped on his hat, snapped his fingers contemptuously at the desk, the cells, and stomped out again, slamming the doors behind him and not giving a damn if the station was no longer manned. It would serve them right if every crook in the country stopped by tonight. But Farley Newstone had had it up to here, and the hell with them all, by god and thunder.

He took the steps to the pavement at a single leap, lifted his head to the rain . . . and never saw the teeth that tore out his throat.

Johanna awoke with a start, wiping sleep away with the backs of her hands while her ears strained in the dark. She had heard something, a whimpering perhaps, or a muffled weeping. At first she wondered if her aunt

was having at last a reaction to the dreadful
news about the death of Uncle Jerad; that
notion was dismissed the moment she re-
called the look on the old woman's face after
she'd been told—it was one of resigned sorrow, shockingly laced with clear relief.

Slowly, she eased her legs over the side of
the down mattress and slipped into a flimsy
peignoir whose satin belt she tied in a loop at
her waist. Barefooted, she hurried to her door
and opened it, listened, and heard the sounds
again.

They were coming from the room at the end
of the short hall; it was Jeddy, and he was
having a nightmare.

Not bothering with a candle, she trotted
down the hall and pushed open the boy's door.
A dim light shifted in through his window
from the streetlamp outside, and she could
see just enough to know he was lying on his
side, covers balled and thrown to the floor;
sweat had drenched him, and he was shivering even as he curled his knees to his chest.
Whimpering sounds came from his tightly
clenched mouth; his hands clutched at the
mattress desperately; his legs suddenly
straightened and made running motions, as if
he were attempting to flee his horrid dreams.

"Oh Jeddy," she whispered, and rushed to
his side, gathered him into her arms and
rocked him.

He did not waken.

But the nightmare passed, and he snuggled
as close as he could, his arms around her

waist, his cheek pressed to her breast. He sighed. His teeth chattered until the chill left him. Once, he whispered his mother's name; once, Elijah MacFarland's.

Johanna soothed him, stroked his matted hair, and stared at the open door.

The rain increased.

She tried to concentrate on only good thoughts, to try somehow to affect the boy's sleep so that he would not be deviled again by what he had witnessed; but she failed miserably. And in failing, fell to pondering all Maria had said that night, and tried to imagine what it might imply.

She knew one thing: that this murderous beast had not drifted out of the woods and come to Oxrun Station by chance. As sure as she breathed, she knew it had deliberately returned here.

Returned.

She held her breath; knowing beyond doubt that the werewolf in human form was someone who lived right here in the village.

And it took her less than five minutes to narrow the field to two names.

Charlie Notting couldn't sleep, not here on the horsehide couch, not here where the lightning flared dimly through the flimsy greying curtains. He tried to blame it on his wife, on the argument they'd had shortly after his return, panting, drenched, bursting through the door in a barely controlled panic.

She began immediately. First she attacked

the way he looked, then for his staying out so long without bothering to have a note sent around to let her know what he was doing, finally scoffing at his story of a supernatural creature stalking the village and letting him know in no uncertain terms that tonight was the last night she would spend under this roof.

He'd said nothing during the tirade, only nodded, shrugged, tried not to look stricken when she lashed out her vow to be shed of him by dawn.

And when she was done, she flounced out of the room, returned a few moments later and tossed a pair of sheets into his arms.

He undressed numbly, lay down and squirmed on the couch willed to him by his father, looked at the furniture willed to him by his father, at the inherited house, at the gloom that seemed to be a permanent fixture of the corners.

He tried to sleep, and blamed his failure on Charlotte.

Finally, after three hours of tossing, thrashing, losing his temper and deciding to storm into the bedroom to take what was legally his, he threw aside the sheets and stood at the window. He wasn't kidding anyone; it wasn't Charlotte who had stolen what rest he needed. It was the beast.

Every time he closed his eyes he saw flecks of amber.

Every time he felt himself drifting, he heard the snorting of the creature as it fed on Don Barrows.

Charlotte had been lost to him a long time ago, and tonight was the first time he was able to admit it. And able to admit that he felt nothing for her, aside from a deep and stinging sadness that they had somehow failed each other.

A vague shrug, and a sigh.

What did it matter? Tomorrow Lucas would ask him to help hunt the beast down, and Charlie wasn't sure what he would say.

He was afraid.

Worse; he was terrified.

He didn't know where he'd get the strength to leave the house.

Claude Drummond lay with his face to the bedroom wall. He was fast asleep. And he was dreaming.

Lawrence Drummond sat in a creaking rocking chair and watched the rain smear the glass of his bedroom window. He dozed and dreamt of wolves, and on his lean face was the faint trace of a smile.

Bartholomew Drummond lay on his bed. He was fully clothed, and his boots were still on. His legs were crossed at the ankles, his hands were cupped beneath his head, and as he stared at the ceiling his lips broke into a smile.

Lucas awoke with a start, punched the air with his fists and kicked at his sheets until he

remembered where he was. Five minutes
passed before he was calm, and another five
minutes before he rolled onto his side, sat up,
and lay clammy hands on his knees. Breathing deeply. Shaking his head to scatter the
last shreds of a dream.

Footsteps in the hallway made his back
rigid, made his head turn slowly as his left
hand reached for the pistol on the nightstand.
A flickering light. A shadow spilling along the
floor. He held his breath, and waited, aiming
at the doorway and listening, listening, until
Maria paused at the threshold. Her robe was
white and worn, her hair still unbraided. A
candle in one hand, a tiny glass in another.

"You cannot sleep," she said softly as she
padded barefoot across the room to sit down
beside him.

He shook his head.

"You are afraid."

He nodded without shame.

The glass found its way into his hand, and
he stared at the dark liquid filled to its brim. A
reluctant smile crossed his face; another one
of her nostrums. For every ill, for every possible occasion, the old woman was able to brew
a potion to cure it, or to make it more bearable.
He never asked what was in any of them; he
wasn't sure he wanted to know.

"You need to rest."

"My god," he said without heat, "how can I?
How . . . can I?"

She poked his arm with a stiff finger. "Tomorrow you are needed, Lucas. Tonight you

must find the strength."

"I don't know, Maria. I don't know what to do."

"Fight."

"Fight what, a ghost? With what, a silver candlestick? How? Shall I line up all the men in the village and touch them with a silver coin to see which of them flinches?"

"Fight," she said simply. "You can do nothing else."

He knew that as he drank the potion down, shuddering at the cloying sweet aftertaste, allowing her to push him down on the bed. The sheet, damp with the perspiration of his nightmare, drifted over him. She leaned down, and tenderly brushed the hair from his face.

"You will do it," she said with a smile, and kissed his forehead. "You will do it, because there is no one else who can."

He wanted to argue, wanted to smack her hand away and call her a meddling old fool; he wanted Johanna to hold him, comfort him, make him promise to do nothing that would cause her to lose him; he wanted to stay here in the dark and wait for the full moon to pass.

The candle flickered away, back to the hall, back to her room.

The rain rattled against the window.

The wind sneered at him from the eaves.

Fight, he thought; and she hadn't answered any of his questions. And when he mulled over what she had said while he readied himself for bed, he wondered how the hell he was going to find out who in the village was responsible for his fear. A man had a pentegram on his palm, or a clutch of dark hairs, or his two middle fingers were of the same length.

So he and his men would go door-to-door and ask to shake hands with everyone inside.

Or he would station men on every corner after sunset, and shoot without asking questions every soul who stepped outside.

Or he would . . .

"Bah!" he muttered, and punched hard at his pillow. "Damn, Lucas, you're not thinking, you're just grasping for straws."

The potion began to work, blurring the edges of his vision, making his head feel light.

Think! he ordered; damn you, man, think!

Suddenly, just as Maria's remedy was about to take hold, he sat upright with an oath so loud he startled himself into clamping a hand over his mouth. A finger rubbed thoughtfully the side of his nose, moved to the center of his forehead and pressed inward, hard.

He had assumed from the moment of his belief's inception that the werewolf had to be someone from Oxrun. It was a sound assumption, since other than the ruffs he had driven off the week before there had been no strangers or visitors brought to his attention, a matter he had always pursued from his first day on the job.

No one came to the Station without his knowledge.

But if Maria was correct, then the werewolf in human form was only recently arrived,

otherwise there would have been killings long
before this; none had occurred in any other
place—that was something else he made a
point of knowing.

The finger moved from his brow to his temple, from his temple to his chin.

That meant it had to be someone who had
been away, and had just returned.

That meant . . .

He stopped himself before he could go further. It was, no matter how he looked at it,
ridiculous. Impossible. Such a thing could not
happen, not to anyone he knew.

amber eyes
howling

He lay back and closed his eyes, grunting
once in an effort to rid himself of the lunacy
that had crept into his mind.

Lawrence Drummond had returned from
the War only five days ago, and his hand from
the beginning had always been buried in his
sling.

Bartholomew Drummond had returned
from Middle Europe only five days ago, and
his hands were encased in white leather
gloves; an affliction, he claimed, a result of
his trip.

Lawrence was bitter; war changes a man,
no question about it, yet it was clear the
younger Drummond had more on his mind
than simply overcoming his wounds.

Bartholomew was uncharacteristically
cold; always an affable if somewhat snobbish
man, this new person baffled everyone, in-

cluding Johanna.

The potion's grip strengthened.

The rain steadied, and lulled him.

And before he fell asleep, he knew who the beast was.

14

Dawn, but no one saw the sun.

The rain continued its pummeling, torrents of clear water spilling over the cobblestones, filling the gutters, flooding yards and lots and falling from roofs in shimmering silver sheets.

The air lightened, but was not light.

The clouds were invisible above the rain.

The temperature continued its inevitable rise, and the bases of trees were the birth-places of serpent-mists, winding over and around roots, slipping into hollows, rearing into the storm only to be beaten down again. Everything was slick and chilled to the touch. And the water drumming on the ground was so constant no one heard it.

In the cellar of the Devon Street cottage Lucas paid no heed to the continuing storm. He was in the far corner reserved as his workshop, bending over a thick iron pot into which he had scraped shavings of the silver candlestick. Heat from the flame beneath bathed his face in perspiration, and the wavering light hollowed his cheeks, deepened the set of his watchful eyes. His expression was grim, his attitude grimly patient.

Further down the table was his Colt Police Model, and a small velvet-lined box for the shells he was making.

A steady hand encased in a thick cotton glove rotated the small pot on its axis while the other rested lightly on his thigh. The flame crawled across the metal; the silver shavings glittered as they softened.

After several long minutes, he straightened, a hand at the small of his back. Then he picked up some toweling and wiped off his face before turning to the candlestick, and picking up his knife.

Not once did he blink as the anniversary gift vanished under the draw of the blade, methodical, relentless.

And he was glad that none of the Council could see him now; they would not have believed, they would have thought him quite insane.

The earthen cellar was cool. The overhead beams laced with cobwebs, strings of roots poking through the walls. A single lantern hung from a chain above his head, swinging slightly when a draught slipped through the slanted double doors that led to the outside behind him.

Nervously, he watched the slivers of metal curl and grow liquid. Time, he thought when the hall clock chimed upstairs; I need more time.

It was already past noon, Maria's potion keeping him abed in a sound, dreamless sleep until nearly eleven. When he awoke, it was instantly; when he clambered out of bed, he felt completely rested, and so enraged at what was happening to his town that he stalked through the house tight-lipped and scowling. Ned avoided him; Maria only glanced at him, and looked away while he ate.

There was no need for words; both knew what had to be done.

Then he had sent Ned to the station, to have Newstone or Charlie wire Hartford to check on the ruffians driven out of Oxrun; there was always a chance, he knew, that one of them might be his quarry, and he did not want a single loose thread dangling from the web before he made his move.

Once Ned had left, he vanished into the cellar, and began his painstaking work.

Now there could be no rush; one small mistake, one tiny bit of imperfection, and all would be lost. And if the beast was not destroyed before the next dawn, he would have to wait another full month, another full month for the killing to start again.

He mopped his face wearily, and did not hear the footsteps coming stealthily down the stairs.

The rain ended shortly after three, not tapering off but stopping abruptly, leaving nothing but drippings from eaves and leaves.

Though the sky did not clear, the sun managed to thin the clouds sufficiently so that the lamplighter was out, snuffing the wicks, turning off the gas, and grumbling to himself.

He was the only one on the street.

Word had already gotten out about Jerad Pendleton, and the failure of the police to locate the killing beast, and not a soul ventured outside; no one wanted to risk meeting the creature, human or otherwise.

Porches were empty, then, yards were clear, the shops on Centre Street seemed filled with ghosts. Every few minutes a breeze touched a tree, and a spray of water dropped from its branches; it was the only sound in the village, aside from the lonely clopping of a horse's hooves as an equally lonely rider made his way from market to home as swiftly as he could.

Deserted; warm; ground fog creeping out of the alleys, out of the earth.

Johanna fussed behind the display counter in Crenshaw's, dusting for the tenth time a tiny silver bowl engraved with grape leaves and patterns of arching olive trees. There hadn't been a single customer in since she'd arrived, and as she looked out onto the street, she shivered. The absense of pedestrians was nearly as unnerving as the thought that the nightbeast would be hunting again tonight.

She had left Jeddy with her aunt, had considered going over to see Lucas and had changed her mind. There was nothing more they could say now, and he would only try to order her back inside, an order they both knew she would dismiss out of hand.

Then Crenshaw came muttering in from the back room and told her she might as well leave for the day; what was the use, the town was spooked. Gratefully, and without comment, she grabbed shawl and purse, and had just stepped out of the door when a white-gloved hand took hold of her arm. She started, covered her mouth to stifle a gasp when she looked up into the eyes of a smiling Bartholomew Drummond.

On Northland Avenue, Charlotte Notting stood at the front door of the Drummond house. She was wearing a bright red dress whose high neckline was edged in stiff lace, whose skirts brushed the stoop thickly, hissing as she shifted impatiently from foot to booted foot. Her hair was fixed in a loose bun, she wore no bonnet, and the only wrap she had was a knitted shawl that hung to a V at the base of her spine. It was a snug dress, one deliberately designed to entice, and to beguile.

She knocked again.

And when the door opened, she began her speech even before she was invited to enter.

Lucas waved Charlie to a stool at the far side of the table, shaking his head to keep the man silent while he slipped a long wooden shaft between two loops on the pot's top; then he positioned the mold and slowly poured the molten silver. The stench wrinkled his nostrils, but his gaze did not waiver until the mold was filled. Then he quickly repositioned the pot, lowered the mold's top, and sat back, sighing loudly.

"Almost done," he said with a weary smile. "Almost done." A look, then, to the younger man, and he raised an eyebrow.

Charlie was wearing a plain brown suit, his collar high and starched, his black tie neatly tied in a very small bow. In his hand he held a round-crowned brown hat. Had it not been for the haunted look in his eyes, he would have appeared perfectly normal.

He reached into a jacket pocket and pulled out a sheet of crumpled paper. "Heard from Hartford," he said, dropping the message onto the table. "Our boys have been in cells since the day they arrived."

Lucas closed his eyes briefly. And shrugged.

"I know," Charlie said. "I'd been hoping myself."

"There's nothing for it now," he said, returning to his work. "But I'll be damned if I know what to do next." He explained, then, what he'd been thinking since dawn, and so intent was he on pouring the next mold that he did not see the hardening of the lines around Charlie's eyes, the rigid set of his mouth. "I suppose I'll have to pay them another visit."

"What will you say?"

"I have no idea. I'll think of something." He chuckled. "Lying was always definitely one of my strong suits, my dad used to tell me."

Charlie rose, and stretched. "I'll be off, then." He was halfway up the rickety stairs when he stopped. "Farley's gone."

"What?" he said without looking around. "What are you talking about?"

"Gone. Left. No sign of him. There was a note on the desk, says he's going to make his fortune in Boston."

"He'll starve and be back by the end of the month."

Charlie watched the steam rise from the stream of silver, and said nothing beyond a meaningless grunt before leaving, before closing the door silently behind him.

Two hours later Lucas tapped the mold lightly and dropped into his hand the last of the silver ammunition. He held it up to the lantern, turned it, examined it, then placed it with the eleven others in the velvet-lined box. Next, he picked up his revolver and began cleaning it asiduously, once, twice, a third time before he was satisfied. Then he took one of the silver bullets and placed it in a chamber, held the Colt up and aimed at the wall. His thumb pulled back the hammer. His eye sighted along the gleaming weapon's barrel.

He pulled the trigger, heard the *click* of the dry-fire, and expelled a held breath before loading the gun completely. The extra ammunition went into the pocket of his white suit jacket, the revolver into his waistband. Then he walked upstairs and into the kitchen.

Maria turned from the basin where she was washing vegetables from the garden.

"You are leaving," she said, her accent suddenly very strong.

"Yes."

She dried her hands on her apron and hurried around the table to take hold of his wrists. "You will be careful," she admonished, then yanked until he was leaning over so she could kiss his cheek soundly. "You will be careful."

He kissed the dry parchment of her brow and walked away, not seeing her lift her hand into a wave that soon flowed into the signing of the Cross over her chest.

He did not seek out Ned; the housekeeper would explain.

And as soon as he hit the outside and took a lungful of fresh air, he felt immensely better. His stride lengthened, his arms swung at his side, and he headed directly for the stationhouse to be sure Charlie was there, to take care of things while he was gone.

While he was hunting.

It was midnight, Johanna thought as she walked apprehensively at Bartholomew's side; it was not yet dinner time and the town felt like midnight.

The streets were still empty, the sky a deep and ominous grey, and by the time they reached Northland Avenue she was trying desperately to think of a way to escape the man's company. Once she had narrowed her targets to two, she'd known almost at once which one it had to be.

She was walking at his side now, and dared not say a word lest he murder her where she stood.

A glance at the white gloves, and her blood turned to ice.

Twice, she attempted to sputter some excuse—her aunt needed her at home during this trying time; little Jeddy needed her support now that his family was gone—but he was too cheerful by half. He spoke of the fear that had gripped the village and mocked it, saying that a few casualties in a war with an overly hungry wolf shouldn't produce an effect like this. It was typical, he declared, of the way Americans had grown soft on the East Coast since the 1812 War. It was all too easy to hide behind locked doors and let someone else do the work.

"That's not fair," she snapped, her tone reminding him that her uncle was one of those casualties he'd mentioned.

"A little harsh, perhaps, yes," he admitted, and laughed. "But it doesn't concern us, does it, my dear. We, you and I, have matters to discuss."

Suspicion made her frown. "What matters, Bart?"

"Why, our nuptials, of course." And he walked four paces on before realizing she had stopped. He turned slowly, grinning. "Jo, have I said something wrong?"

"Indeed you most certainly have," she told him sternly. "I've never agreed to marry you, Bart. I've never even given you cause to think so."

"Of course you haven't," he said, returning to take her arm again. "But I am exercising a bit of foresight, a little planning. I never do anything on the spur of the moment."

"And you aren't going to marry me that

way, either."

He laughed again, his humor so infectious that she forgot her nervousness and laughed with him, shaking her head in wonder at his persistence . . . until she remembered the gloves on his hands.

"And now," he said grandly as they reached the corner, "I have a surprise for you."

"Oh?"

"Yes," he said. "I am taking you home, Johanna Pendleton. My home, that is."

"Now wait, Bart—"

"No arguments, my dear," he said, tightening his grip slightly. "No arguments, please. There is something there I want you to see."

15

LUCAS STOOD BEHIND the front desk and glared at the sheet of paper squared on the brown blotter. Charlie had told him Newstone had left a farewell note, but this couldn't be it. The right words were there, but the handwriting was all wrong. It was cramped, almost illegible, and the message was so terse it defied all he knew about the missing man.

He picked up the sheet and tore it in half, tore it again and dropped the pieces on the floor.

Hovering by the railing were three of his men, and none had the faintest idea where Farley had gone, or, in fact, where Charlie was now. They hadn't seen Newstone since coming on duty this morning, and Charlie had rushed in and rushed out only a while ago without saying a word.

Damn you, Notting, he thought; you're going to get yourself killed.

He reached for his hat, changed his mind, and stepped off the platform. The others backed away as he strode through the gate and headed for the doors. A command snapped over his shoulder kept them from following; an oath for the empty street was brushed aside by the wind.

He paused on the top step to adjust the revolver more comfortably in his waistband, pulled his waistcoat down, drew his cut-away jacket closed over his stomach. Then he fairly marched across the street without bothering to check for traffic, turned into Northland Avenue and headed for the Drummonds.

Farley was dead; he was sure of it.

Charlie was off to avenge the sullying of his wife.

He shook his head as he reached the iron fence, shook it again when he pushed through the gate and stormed up the walk. He cautioned himself to be calm, not to give the game up before he had a chance to start it, and he had to stand for several seconds on the stoop in order for his mind to stop its swirling.

He knocked twice, three times, and still, after a fourth summons, no one came to the door.

When he tried the latch, the door swung open, and he called out as he stepped over the threshold into the foyer.

The house was silent and smelled of must, as if no one had lived there for a century or more.

He called out again, Larry's name, Bart's,

as he poked his head into each of the rooms on the first floor. Part of him noted the expensive furnishings he passed, part of him noted the gold and silver ornamentation lying freely about, and part of him noted a familiar scent in the air, one he could not place though it taunted his memory and made him scowl, clench his fists.

He took a deep breath, closed his eyes and tried to force the identification into the open. When it failed, he put it aside; it would come eventually; right now, he hadn't the time.

At the staircase he looked up, one hand on the bannister. If the old man was awake, surely he would have heard him. Suddenly, fear for Claude Drummond's safety had him running, taking the steps two at a time, reaching the top panting as he veered to his left and rushed down the carpeted hall toward the door at the far end, slightly ajar.

He knocked on the frame, cocked his head and listened.

Knocked again, and pushed the door from him.

The old man was sitting in his rocking chair, its back to the window. A blanket was draped snugly over his legs, and a plate of untouched food was on the floor by his side.

"Mr. Drummond?"

Though the light was fading rapidly behind him, the old man was little more than a dark figure against the pane. He stirred at his name, the rocker creaked, his slippered feet shifted.

"Mr. Drummond, it's Lucas Stockton."

"Well, so it is," Claude Drummond said. "Well, I'll be damned, so it is."

Lucas took a single step into the room uninvited, took it all in a single glance and tried not to show his horror.

He had seen cleaner stables, had smelled lovelier compost heaps. No wonder the old man never got well; the way his sons were treating him, it was a miracle he was still alive. Wallpaper hung in strips of varying length, different colors exposed to the gloom as though slapped on haphazardly, without thought, without care; the carpeting was similarly torn and worn, and the pegged flooring in great patches appeared to be gouged; what he first thought were clumps of dust were on closer inspection lumps of rotted food.

"Not pretty, is it," Drummond said dryly.

"I'm sorry, sir, but it's . . . it's a disgrace."

Drummond laughed, a harsh rasping that made Lucas frown and look up. At least, he thought, the old man sounded in decent health.

The rocker creaked as Drummond shifted. His blanket slipped off his knees, and Lucas made a move to replace it. "Don't bother, don't bother," the old man said irritably. "It's too warm anyhow. I don't like it. Never did." He snorted, sniffed, tilted his head to one side. "What can I do for you, Chief? It is Chief now, isn't it? I was told that. Chief now, good for you. So what can I tell you? You think I robbed someone's house?"

The laugh again, stronger.

"Your sons," Lucas told him. "I'm looking for your sons."

"So am I, Chief Stockton. I've been looking for them for years."

He shrugged the bitterness off without moving, instead glanced over his shoulder at the hallway behind. "I . . . I need to talk with them, sir," he said, trying not to gag at the odors assaulting his nostrils. "I believe they have information about something I'm investigating."

"Ah, the beast," the old man said cheerfully. "You're hunting the wild beast and you think the boys can tell you about it?"

"Something like that, sir, yes."

"I see, I see." The rocker moved faster, the shadow-man lunging toward him, dropping away. "Well, I don't know where they are," he snarled petulantly. "They never tell me their comings and goings, and I don't want to know. They are on their last legs in this house, I don't mind telling you, Chief Stockton, and if they never come back it will be too soon for me. Too soon. The bastards."

Lucas fussed absently with the bow of his tie, smoothed a hand over his waistcoat. "Well, sir," he said gamely, "if you should—"

"I'll tell them, I'll tell them," Drummond assured him grumpily. "And if you see them two idiots first, tell them I'm still waiting."

Lucas backed to the doorway, concern for the man's condition overriding distaste at his temper. "Mr. Drummond . . ." He paused,

hoping the man wouldn't take offense. "Mr.
Drummond, is there something I can get for
you? Food? Drink? Do you have medicine in
the house?" He looked around the filthy room,
barely contained a gasp when he saw the bolts
and locks lining the inside of the door. "Shall I
fetch John Webber?"

"John Webber is a fool," Drummond
sneered. "I have no need of anything, thank
you, Chief Stockton. On my own time I am
getting well, believe it or not."

He didn't, but he saw no reason to contra-
dict the old man. He merely nodded his
thanks, and hurried back down the hall as
fast as he could, fairly leapt down the staircase and had to stop for a moment in the foyer
to keep himself from bolting through the front
door.

Johanna, he thought then, can defend those
two as much as she will, but after what he
had seen today, he would never be more than
coldly civil to them again. And despite what
the old man wanted, he was going to send for
John Webber as soon as he could; no man, not
even the cantankerous Drummond, deserved
to be penned up in his own house like that.

The door closed behind him.

He looked up.

It was night.

As an afterthought, and though uncertain
he was doing the right thing, Lucas turned
left after leaving the gate and headed for King
Street. Since Charlie was not at the Drum-

monds, and since neither of the brothers was in the house, there was still a chance the young man had returned home to confront his wife. When he reached the house, however, he faltered. A light shone in the front window, and he could see a shadow moving back and forth across the curtains.

His hesitation lasted but a moment; then he took the broken flagstone walk to the door and pounded on it, hoping that whatever altercation was going on inside would wither at the sound.

Charlie answered the door, still nattily dressed though his hair and beard were in violent diasarry as though he had been clawing through them.

"She's gone," he said when he saw who his visitor was. "She's gone, run away with Lawrence Drummond." Then he gave a helpless shrug. "I'm a fool. I know. It wasn't until I got back here, ready to strangle them both, that I realized I'm better off without her." His smile was painful to see; Lucas sighed and shook his head. "I really did act the fool, didn't I, Lucas?"

"No more fool than any other man in love the way you were," he said. And as he waited for Charlie to fetch his hat and gun, he said, "How do you know it was Lawrence? Is there a note?"

"Yes, but she only said she was leaving me for a Drummond. I . . . I went there to have it out with them, and couldn't raise anyone. And when I saw Bartholomew walking Miss Pendleton along the street, I just did a simple subtraction."

Lucas's eyes widened. "You saw Jo?"

"Well, yes," Charlie said as they walked out the door. "They were . . ." He stopped, and slapped his forehead. "My god!"

Lucas was already off and running, jacket tails slapping the air behind him, boots harsh on the pavement. An exchange of grim glances was the only communication between them until they reached Chancellor Avenue. Then Lucas spun to a halt and shoved Charlie toward the station.

"We can't take any chances," he said to the man's bewildered look. "You roust the men, then see what you can do to find Charlotte. If we're wrong, she's the one in danger. No matter what you feel now, Charlie, you've got to do what you can to help her."

He didn't wait for Charlie's nod; he sprinted across the street and headed for the Inn. Dinner, he thought, locking onto the only reason he could think of why Bartholomew hadn't brought her directly to his house; he's lured her with a fancy dinner, some wine, and . . .

His palm hit the door and slammed it open. Those in the bar quieted instantly, those in the lefthand dining room took only a second more to interrupt their conversations, look around, and stare.

"I'm looking for Bartholomew Drummond and Johanna Pendleton," he bellowed, hands on his hips. "I'm looking for them now!"

A second's buzzing before heads began to shake.

A waiter was snared on his way up the stairs, and he was told that the couple was not up there either.

He whirled and ran out again, not caring what they thought about his behavior, feeling only an abiding deep cold settle around his heart.

Bartholomew stood uneasily in the Pendleton parlor, watching as Delia fawned about him, waiting for Johanna to return with the boy. He'd planned something entirely different for this evening, but she'd prevailed upon him to include Jeddy in their party as well, something, she said, to get his mind off his troubles.

When they returned, the boy tucked under her arm and staring open-mouthed at him, he smiled.

"Gee," the boy said, shifting his stare to the white gloves, "are your hands really coming off like the other kids say?"

"Jeddy!" Johanna scolded, and cuffed the boy's ears.

Delia scurried into the kitchen, not wanting to witness her niece's last chance for success drowned in disgrace.

Bartholomew laughed heartily, however, and knelt in front of him. "I'm starving, m'boy, but I think dinner can wait for just one more minute."

Johanna looked out the window, and saw

the first faint glow of the moon. In the hand she'd kept behind her back was the silver bowl she'd secreted from Crenshaw's shop.

"Take a look, boy," Bartholomew said sternly. "Take a good look."

And he stripped off his gloves.

16

"I DON'T UNDERSTAND," Charlotte whispered, drawing the shawl more snugly around her head and bare shoulders. "What are we waiting for?" When Lawrence didn't respond, she pouted but said nothing more. There was no sense spoiling the perfection of her dream-come-true, no sense in antagonizing the man when he had agreed to everything she'd demanded. She had known he would, but when he had answered the door she could not help feeling that perhaps she had made a mistake, had overestimated his willingness to take her away from the Station.

But he had taken her inside while she was still delivering her ultimatum, laved her face with eager kisses, and virtually dragged her into the front room where they shared a quiet glass of wine. Their eyes had done all the talking for them, and by the time her glass was empty she knew that she had him.

Then suddenly it had all gone wrong.

Just before nightfall, he had grown increasingly nervous, fidgeting in his chair, snapping his fingers, finally rising on his crutch and asking her to come outside with him. For all that was involved, she had no qualms about obeying; later, when he was all hers in a place all their own, she would lay down the law. For now she would follow him meekly.

This, however, was not what she had in mind.

They were crouched behind the tool shed, back of the house, and Lawrence had grown unnaturally silent. Her few attempts to draw him out had failed miserably, and when he finally did speak, she was so startled she gasped.

"Do you know what it's like to be dead?" he asked, keeping his gaze on the dark windows.

"W–what?"

"Do you know what it's like to suffer, Charlotte?"

"Don't be silly," she whispered. "My whole life—"

A hand clamped hard over her mouth, shook her head until an ache sprang up at her nape. She struggled to free herself, was ready to bite into his palm when just as abruptly the hand fell away.

"Now listen here, Lawrence Drummond," she began, but he hushed her with a black look, took her hand and led her around the shed toward the back door.

"You want me to take you away," he said as

they moved through the dark, as the moon rose above trees.

She nodded.

"You want me to spend a fortune on you, is that it?"

Denying it was futile; he was much too canny for that.

"Then just this once, my darling, you must do as I say. Just this once, and we'll have father's carriage and be on our way before dawn."

He opened the door and slipped in, a moment later reached out and pulled her in with him, indicated the back stairs to the second floor and gave her a gentle shove.

"Go up," he whispered. "It's all right. My room is the first on the right."

She grinned wickedly; this bit of entertainment she hadn't exactly counted on. Not loathe to tempt the fates in the Drummonds' very house, however, she nodded with a giggle.

"I will be up in a moment," he said when she paused. "There is something I must do first. Don't worry. I'll be along."

The mere thought of him touching her, kissing her, in his own bed made her flesh tighten, and she hurried up the narrow staircase, pulling herself along on a thin, polished bannister. Who would have thought that a man ruined by war could be so satisfying a lover? Who would have thought it of a Drummond even if he were whole; and she barely contained another burst of giggling as she reached the door and eased it open.

The hallway was bleak, broken here and there by spills of growing moonlight that lay on the carpet. It seemed oddly cold, and she dropped the shawl from her hair to cover the expanse of her breasts, frowned until she remembered he'd said the room was on the left.

Holding her breath, then, she stepped out of the doorway, and heard something breathing harshly in the dark.

"It's certainly something to tell all your little friends, isn't it," Bartholomew said solemnly as he pulled his gloves back on.

Johanna felt slightly faint, and swallowed at the foul taste that had climbed out of her throat.

Aunt Delia had not returned; the room was growing dark.

"Unfortunately, the disease has no name that I can readily pronounce," the man explained with an apologetic gesture to them both. "But I can assure you, little man, that it is neither painful, nor infectious. And don't worry," he added, "you won't catch it. I promise."

He grinned mirthlessly down at the small boy cringing at Johanna's skirts, as though he'd expected the youth to have more courage.

"It is, quite frankly, more a nuisance than anything else," he continued, holding his hands up to smooth the white leather down toward his wrists. "The gloves are specially lined and carry a salve which soothes and renews the skin should it become irritated."

"Bart," Johanna warned, clutching the boy to her, "I think he's had enough."

A wink, then, and he reached out slowly to pat Jeddy's head. "Is that so, Jedadiah Tripper? Are you really satisfied now?"

"Don't touch me!" the boy yelled tearfully, and before Johanna could stop him he had dashed from the room.

"That was cruel of you, Bart," Johanna snapped. "He's just a little boy."

"Little boys must learn things," he answered coolly. "And when they are so boldy curious like your little friend, very often it's the hard way."

She wanted to say more but couldn't. The sight of the man's hands—a sullen red and covered with tiny white flakes of dead skin that fell to the carpet even as he thrust them toward Jeddy—had produced a double reaction within her: one was relief she'd seen no symptoms that would brand him the night-beast, the other a churning revulsion mixed with sympathy for his plight.

Nevertheless, she could also not help being annoyed at the way he had treated Jeddy.

He rose to his full height then, and looked in the direction the boy had taken. "Am I right in assuming, Johanna, that he is not coming with us."

"Yes," she said flatly. "And I'm afraid neither am I."

He swung his gaze back, the dead smile still at his lips. "Oh, but I'm afraid you must, my dear."

She shook her head firmly. "I've had quite

enough of you for this evening, Bart. I thank you for the invitation, but I'm going to have to decline."

He sighed, and looked around the sparsely furnished room. "I feel I must insist."

"Insist all you want," she told him, wondering what was preventing Delia from returning from the back. "I'm still not going."

An eyebrow lifted. "You have a temper, Johanna, and a mind of your own. I suppose you think that admirable in this day and age."

She glared at him, one foot tapping impatiently on the floor.

"Is it perhaps the illustrious Chief of Police? Could he be the one who rivals me for your affection?"

"There is no question of rivalry, Bart. My affection is his, and his alone. Now please, before Aunt Delia returns, I must ask you to leave."

Sadly, he turned and walked to the door, had his hand out on the knob before he looked back. "Are you sure, Johanna? After all, I haven't even begun the best part of the courtship. It really will be fun, you know. Well, perhaps not exactly fun, but you won't find it dull."

"My . . . *god!*" she exploded. "Has your . . . your illness affected your ears as well? Bartholomew, I have no intention of being the object of anything of yours, much less your courtship. Now for heaven's sake, will you please leave?"

Regret passed his features, and he slipped his free hand into his jacket.

"Bartholomew—"

And it came back into the light grasping a silver-handled derringer.

Her eyes widened in disbelief, and she took one step back, her hands up, palms out. "This . . . this isn't funny anymore, Bart. Please put that thing away."

"Oh I will," he said. "Just as soon as you agree that it's in your best interest to accompany me."

She blinked.

"Now, Johanna!" he said, and straightened his arm, aimed the weapon at her chest. "Now, my dear. We've no time to waste."

Charlotte huddled back against the wall, holding her breath as the dark figure rose out of the front stairwell and headed directly for her. She looked wildly around for Lawrence, then thrust herself away and started running for his bedroom door. Footsteps thumped behind her, a hand snared her arm, and before she could scream a palm was clamped to her mouth.

"Hush!" someone said in her ear. "Damnit, woman, don't say a word!"

She struggled for several seconds before recognizing the voice, and she twisted her neck around to look straight into Charlie's eyes. He waited a moment longer before uncovering her mouth, but he did not release her arm.

"What the hell are you doing here?" she demanded loudly, then glanced guiltily over her shoulder. "What do you want?"

"Not you," he said grimly, pulling her toward the staircase. "Don't think I've come to take you back."

"A good thing, because I'm not . . . going," and she wrenched her arm free, causing him to stagger away. "Now get out of here, Charlie Notting, before Lawrence comes back and I'm forced to have him thrash you."

He refused, and reached for her again. She backed away, glowering, and wondering what had gotten into him, what was keeping her lover.

"Damnit, Charlotte, listen to me," he said. "You don't know what you've gotten yourself into."

"Oh Charlie," she sighed. "Charlie, can't you understand that—"

"Hush! Damn you, shut your mouth!"

Startled into silence by the vehemence of his command, she froze in the center of the hall, seeing him pull out his revolver and pull the hammer back. Now this, she thought, was too much indeed. It was all very nice he still loved her enough to want to murder poor Lawrence, but this . . . this was carrying things just a little too far.

She took a step toward him, one hand out to take the gun, when she saw another shadow down at the far end of the hall. At last, she thought; at last you've come.

"Lawrence—"

The shadow stepped into the square of moonlight cast on the floor.

Charlie groaned.

Charlotte couldn't believe her eyes, and fell back against the wall with the back of one hand covering her mouth.

It was huge, and white, and its fangs dripped saliva onto the carpet while its hideous amber eyes fixed first on her, then her husband with its malevolent gaze.

The roar of Charlie's gun deafened her, and made her scream; the roar of the nightbeast buckled her knees and sent her sliding to the floor.

Charlie fired again, twice more, before the creature launched itself at him, and she could feel its passage as it swept through the air and landed on Charlie's chest. He shrieked, and tried to pummel its skull with his weapon; it growled, and bayed, and tore his chest open with its teeth.

The hall darkened then as Charlotte drew her knees to her breast and buried her face in her skirts.

Snarling, cries for help, the sound of flesh tearing, the sound of bones snapping.

She wept, screamed again, finally shook her head violently and began crawling toward the back stairs. Charlie called out to her, but she couldn't help him: Charlie screamed high-pitched and long until the sound was mixed with blood and air gurgling in his throat.

Oh God, she thought; oh God oh God please help me please help me please . . .

Something slammed against her back, lifted her from the floor and she crashed into the wall. Dazed, her head spinning with pain, she rubbed a hand over her eyes as she fought to regain her feet.

Charlie was silent.

She gulped for air, and lowered her hand.

And found herself looking straight at the nightbeast's fangs.

17

"DELIA PENDLETON . . . !"

Lucas raised a quivering fist over his head, would have brought it down gladly on the simpering, hysterical woman had not Jeddy burst out of the kitchen, sobbing and throwing himself into his arms. Within moments he managed to piece together what had happened between Johanna and Bartholomew, and with an outraged look to Jo's aunt for complaining about his lack of protection for the village the moment he walked into the house instead of warning him of the danger her niece was in, he cautioned both of them to remain inside, bolt the doors, turn out the lights.

Then he was gone, revolver springing to hand as he dashed into the street and headed for the Drummond house.

Castigating his own shortsightedness, he fumbled in his waistcoat pocket for the shrill

police whistle to summon his men from the
station, or their beats. And changed his mind.
What good would it do? He had no time to
explain what they were up against, and their
own weapons would be useless against the
nightbeast he was after.

There was also a brief moment of self-
denigration when he realized that he should
have known all along it was Lawrence, not
Bart. Bart was the obvious one, the one who
had traveled through Europe, had been to
Maria's territory; Lawrence, on the other
hand, was only, he had thought, a victim of
the country's own terrible war.

God, he thought angrily; how could a man
be so horribly wrong!

But wrong he certainly was, and it wasn't
too farfetched to believe that Bartholomew
knew it all, and had come to some sort of
demonic pact with his inflicted brother. How
the man had been transformed from human
to werewolf was a question he might never be
able to answer, but that was secondary now to
saving Johanna's life.

Pelting across Chancellor, he had to swerve
sharply to avoid being struck by the Harley
coach, and the driver yelled epithets at him,
swung out his whip and would have caught
the top of his head had not the horses reared
at the commotion and thrown off his aim.

He stumbled on the slick cobblestone as he
rounded sharply into Northland.

The clouds above had been driven off by the
force of the nightwind that parted them,
shredded them, cleared the sky for the stars,

and the last night of the full moon.

He looked up as he ran, and looked away quickly. An object once of amazement and wonderment, now it filled him with terror at what its cold light could produce.

Heels loud and echoing; breath loud and gasping.

A dog barked at him fiercely from behind someone's fence, and he swung his gun around, just barely holding fire when he saw what it was; a cat hissed when he slipped as he jumped the curbing and fell into a rain-laden hedge; a horseman slowed back at the intersection and watched in puzzlement, called out to ask if he needed any help.

By the time he reached the iron fencing he had to use it to pull himself along while he kept his gaze on the house itself, on the light that shone from the top window, center.

When the gate didn't give immediately, he vaulted it without effort; when he leapt to the stoop he didn't bother to knock—he slammed the door open and stood panting in the foyer.

The house was quiet, overly warm, the wind slipping in behind him stirring fringes and curtains, the moon creating a long shadow that stretched before him to the stairs.

He could smell it then; he could smell the fresh blood.

Not knowing which way to turn, he was about to call out Johanna's name when he heard voices, urgent low voices drifting down the stairwell. Quietly pulling back the hammer, cocking the trigger, he began to climb, testing each step for betrayal before moving to the next.

By the time he was halfway up he could hear them, arguing.

"You're a fool! How could you do this, bringing them here for the kill. Do you want to have the entire place down around our heads?"

"Brother, if you'll stop ranting for a moment and give me a hand, we can take care of this."

"Of course, certainly, let me do all the work."

"Well, I'm hardly in a position to carry them myself."

The sound of grunting, and something heavy scraping across the floor.

"This is insane."

"Shut up, Bart, he'll hear you."

"I never should have . . ."

"Damn you, man, hold your tongue! And be careful, you'll drop her."

"Slut. She was only a slut."

A low rumbling laugh. "If she could only see herself now, eh, Bart? If she could see . . ."

"Enough, Lawrence, that's enough. Let's just get it done."

A door opening on hinges badly wanting oil.

The voices muffled for a moment, then clear once again as they returned to the hallway.

"Now him."

"Do him yourself. I've got to get the girl and . . ."

"She'll wait, brother, she'll wait. She's not going anywhere, at least not tonight."

"She'll wake up soon. I don't want her screaming her fool head off."

The laugh again, this time mocking. "A bit much for you, was she? I could have told you that. Old Charlotte was a pushover compared to that one, believe me."

Again the sound of something being dragged awkwardly across the hall.

"I didn't know there was supposed to be seven."

"What's the difference after the first one?"

"Lawrence, you're disgusting."

"No, just practical. I want that money just as badly as you. In fact, probably worse. You can always make more because you're good at that sort of thing."

"You would be too if you weren't so damned simpering."

"You got me into this."

"You agreed. You didn't have to."

"Bart, there are times when I'd like to kill you as well."

Lucas had heard enough. Disgust at their bickering even in the midst of all that death lifted him from his crouched position on the top step, had his hand reaching for the gaslight on the wall by his head. He turned the beveled knob, and the light glowed sharply, and he had to bite down on his lip to prevent himself from gagging.

Lawrence and Bartholomew Drummond were standing in front of an open door midway along the hall; Lawrence was holding Charlie's bloodied head, Bartholomew his feet. Lucas did not have to look closely to see the gap in his friend's chest, or the thickening pools of blood that darkened the carpet.

The two looked up, startled, dropped the corpse as one and Lawrence kicked shut the door.

"Good evening," Lucas said.

Bartholomew, with a wild look of desperation, reached into his pocket and pulled out his derringer. Lucas didn't bother to order him to stop; he aimed straight at the man's chest and gladly pulled the trigger.

The gun's retort was loud in the narrow hall, Bartholomew's body thrown back against the wall. He looked down at the hole in his shirt, at the blood seeping through, silently begged his brother for assistance as he crumpled to the floor.

"Very nice," Lawrence said, raising his free hand over his head. "Good shooting, Chief. I'll commend you to God the next time I see Him."

"Where is Johanna?"

Lawrence smiled. "Johanna who?"

Lucas cocked the hammer again, and aimed at the man's head. "I'll do it, Drummond, don't think I won't. For all you've done to this town I will gladly put a bullet into your brain if you don't tell me where she is."

For the first time, Drummond seemed indecisive. He looked at his dead brother, then down at the young constable sprawled at his feet. A hand brushed resignedly back through his hair.

"It was too good to last, I suppose. Sooner or later someone would believe, and it would be all over."

"Johanna," he repeated flatly. "Tell me where you've put her."

Drummond jerked a thumb over his shoulder, pointing to the room at the end of the hall.

Lucas couldn't believe it; they had put her in with their father. He took a deep breath to keep control of his embroiled emotions, then gestured angrily with the Colt, moving Lawrence ahead of him. The man obeyed with a slight shrug, his crutch banging on the floor as he limped toward the door. Lucas followed, closing his eyes briefly when he skirted the body of Charlie Notting.

"It was that stupid old woman, wasn't it?" Drummond guessed as he moved ahead of Lucas's shadow. "That housekeeper of yours. She's the one who put you onto it, wasn't she? Told you all the stories about werewolves and things."

"Yes," he said, then raised his voice. "Johanna, can you hear me? It's Lucas. Lucas Stockton."

Relief almost made him lower his gun when he heard her muffled cry. They had probably gagged her, but at least she was still alive.

"The hero," Drummond said when he reached the door, suddenly turned and shook his head. "How does it feel to be a hero, Chief? Feel all good and cozy inside?"

His finger tightened on the trigger; Drummond saw it and winced, tensed for the impact, and did not relax when the gun did not fire.

"The seven," Lucas said then, motioning the man to one side. "What did you mean about the seven."

Lawrence giggled, hiccoughed, and covered his mouth. Close to him now, Lucas could see the glint of sly madness full in his eyes.

"Seven hearts, my dear Chief. Seven hearts to fill the gullet, and keep the dear diner young."

"Christ, how could you do it, Larry?" he blurted. "My god, man, what made you do it?"

"Why, the money, of course," Drummond said, rocking slowly on his good foot while the crutch described tiny circles over the blood-stained carpet. "The money, the money, it's always the money."

Lucas frowned; he didn't understand.

"The money, you idiot," Drummond said in disdain. "A man will do just about anything for half a million in gold."

Lucas straddled the threshold, looked in and saw Johanna trussed and gagged on the bed. She was sitting up against the wall, her head shaking side to side. He looked back to Drummond, and motioned him ahead of him. And once inside he saw the old man in his rocking chair, still backed against the window.

"What about the gold," he demanded as he covered Lawrence with the gun and moved to untie Johanna with his free hand. "I still don't get it, about the gold."

"You really are stupid," Lawrence said, giggling louder. "Stupid, stupid, stupid."

Suddenly, he lunged for the revolver, and Lucas had no choice but to fire pointblank into his chest. He shrieked, his momentum carrying him forward, dropping him to the floor just before he reached the bed. Lucas, his anger at what they'd done to Johanna poisoning his reason, fired again, and again, directly into the man's back.

Then he sagged, energy spent, without even the strength to look at the old man for forgiveness.

Johanna, meanwhile, was struggling, kicking her feet to gain his attention. Finally, like a man roused from a deep sleep, he yanked at the knots, pulled them free at last, and was astonished when she slapped his hand away and pulled free the gag.

"Lucas!" she shouted. "For god's sake, it's not him!"

"Indeed," said Claude Drummond.

And rose from his chair.

Taller, wider, the light from the hallway giving Lucas a perfect view when the old man began the *change*.

Johanna screamed.

Claude Drummond snarled, casting aside his shawl and blanket as his body twisted and writhed, tore through his shabby clothes, rippling black to white while his eyes *changed* to amber.

Lucas climbed onto the bed and thrust Johanna behind him. It was impossible, it was Lawrence who was supposed to be the enemy, not an old man held prisoner in his own room. Lawrence, he thought wildly, it was Lawrence, damnit, Lawrence.

The thing that had been Claude Drummond

lifted its head, and howled.

The thing that needed one heart more swayed like a serpent coiling to strike.

Then the gun fired, and the nightbeast was slammed backward into the rocker, which caught its legs and spun it around while Lucas blindly fired again.

And this time the bullet entered the back of its head, propelled it against the window sill, still howling its rage, screaming its pain . . . glass shattering . . . the nightbeast howling . . . Drummond falling to the ground two stories below.

18

"I AM OF the perfectly sound opinion," Lucas said for the hundredth time that September, "that I shall never permit a dog into my house."

He was walking along the main path of Oxrun's park, his white suit long since discarded for one of dark brown tweed. He did not wear a hat, and his revolver was nesting unobtrusively in a holster beneath his left arm.

"Well, if you want my opinion—"

"Which I don't."

"—you are being absolutely unreasonable," Johanna said, ignoring the interruption. "There's nothing wrong with a dog, nothing at all. Give it a year, and you'll soon change your mind."

He laughed, albeit uncertainly, and hugged her arm close to his side. It was a beautiful day, the leaves beginning to change from

green to the rainbow, the grass still rich, the
children playing in the field to their right
lifting high laughing voices into the chill twi-
light air.

Oxrun Station was back to normal, and he
had been spared the task of trying to convince
his neighbors that they had been stalked by a
creature spawned of a hellish dream. The
official verison of the crimes' solving declared
that the Drummond brothers, in conspiracy
against their father, had brutally murdered
anyone they suspected of getting in their way.
At the end, before Lucas could stop them, they
had struggled with the old man and he'd
fallen from the window, all because they
were impatient to gain the family fortune.

Most believed it. Those who doubted kept
their silence.

Lucas, however, had spent many long
nights puzzling it out, and had finally, with
Johanna's aid, come to the conclusion that it
was the brothers' surliness and disdain for
them all that blinded them to the common
knowledge that Claude had been to Europe as
well. And there, he surmised, the old man had
been bitten, had returned ahead of his sons
and had in the resulting madness locked himself in his room.

When Lawrence came back from the War,
when Bartholomew returned from the Tour,
he promised them each a half million dollars
in gold if they would keep his secret, help him
find victims; the seven hearts supposedly
would restore his youth to him.

Jerad had died more tragically than the

rest; he had simply been in the wrong place at the wrong time.

The young Tripper was lucky. When he'd seen the beast that night on his father's farm, he had fainted dead away, and for some unknown reason the beast had passed him up. When he awoke later, he crawled immediately into his secret hiding place to wait for rescue.

Now he lived happily with Johanna.

They paused at a break in the shrubbery that lined the path, and Johanna lay her head against his arm. Above them, the sky was indigo, shading to black, and the moon was climbing over the park's low hill.

"Lovely," she said.

Lucas shuddered. "I still can't look at it without . . . well, you know what I mean."

"My Lucas," she sighed. "The world's chief worrier, and the world's only protector."

"Jo, that's not fair."

"No," she said, "But you're so easy to tease, Lucas, I can't resist it."

A gang of children swept past them shouting, and on the other side of the open grassy expanse they could see Aunt Delia hustling toward them, skirts flaring.

"Oh lord," he groaned, "what's the boy done now?"

"Nothing at all, if I know her," she said. Delia had agreed only reluctantly to taking in the child, and had had her hands full ever since. His energy was boundless, and she complained to anyone who would listen that he would put her in an early grave.

"Lucas," Johanna said then, not taking her eyes off her aunt, "Do you remember what you told me last month?"

He stiffened. "I told you a lot of things last month, if you recall."

"I mean, after I said that Bart had proposed."

"Oh." He sniffed, and fussed with the knot of his tie. "Oh, that."

"Yes, that," she laughed, slapping him lightly on the chest. "And I want to know if you're going to make an honest woman of me. I warn you, if you don't I'll have a word with Delia."

At that moment Delia confronted them, huffing, red-faced, pointing wordlessly back across the field.

"What is it?" Lucas asked, not really caring. "Where's Jeddy?"

"I don't know, and I don't care," the old woman said. Then she held up her hand. "That little bastard bit me."

On Devon Street, behind the Stockton cottage, beyond the slow dying garden, Maria Andropayous knelt fearfully on the cold ground and uttered a short prayer.

In the light of the full moon . . .

. . . the wolfsbane was blooming.